The Found Diary
of
Avery
Alexander Myer

M. A. Fink

Illustrations by Gromyko Semper

www.tornadoskin.com

ISBN: 0615592457

ISBN-13: 978-0615592459

To Gabriel, Michelle, Pan and Mircea.

Acknowlegements

Thanks to Dee Kern for support during the fitfull writing of this story, to Mary Scherr for help while the editing and illustrations were coming together, and to Jean Vengua for actively (if carefully) prodding me to give the whole thing form. Thanks to my graphic designer Kate Reed and my illustrator Gromyko Semper. Without the dedication of Rusty Hodge of Soma.FM to provide commercial-free music 24 hours a day, the tone of this novel might have been very different.

This story first appeared serially on Livejournal between 2004 and 2006.

Aug. 11th, 2004 09:25 pm Entry 1

I finally found some paper.

I'm not going to be able to write much before I pass out, but the presence of pen and paper, along with light in the form of a couple of fat white candles, has given me a stone to stand on amidst... whatever it is I'm going through.

The food helped, too, it must be said.

My hand is already shaking. It's been quite a while between meals, so I'm weak (as a blind kitten, my mother quipped inside my head, msrip). I also fear I'm dehydrated. I can't bring myself to drink the water (yet). The meal I just had—of crackers, potted meat and dried pears—will probably change my mind soon. It was the first food in two days, though; I used to hate potted meat ("potted meat"—I said it out loud), but now I think I'm deeply in love with it. Deeply, deeply. God, I'm tired. Thanks for the paper, you bastard.

More tomor

Aug. 12th, 2004 02:57 pm Entry 2

...row. I actually fell asleep while writing. I have not done that since school.

School was a long time ago.

14 hours of sleep later, I quickly figured out how to use the crazy-huge compost toilet. Either it had not been used in a long time, or it works very well, as there was no hint of odor. There is a tight stack of magazines squashed into an iron rack next to the toilet. It's funny—I desperately want clues to where I am or what has happened to me, but I have a perverse aversion to reaching for the magazines, or even of searching through the house I found last night. I think I might still be in shock. Maybe I just want to clear my head first, before putting any more into it?

So instead, I just came back from an inordinate amount of time scouting the area outside, now that it is broad daylight. You'd think I would want to stay indoors after two days of stumbling about in the elements.

I seem to have found myself a quaint white house. It has no path, road or walkway up to it. It sits in a friendly manner on a rolling plain covered in short yellow-green grass, dotted here and there with scruffy weeds a little like stubby saw-grass. The whole landscape seems rather arid.

It was not too long before I discovered the cliffs. Almost due east from the house (House) the grassland drops off abruptly, straight down to a thin strip of beach. That, of course, then becomes a shoreline, but I'm not ready to write about that, yet.

Or about the statue.

I need to eat a little and close my eyes.

I'm wide awake at midnight, by myself in a strange house. There is no electricity, nor even any outlets. I have 28 candles lit. It's so dark outside. I just realized I haven't seen a moon, yet. I meant: the Moon, yet.

start over Avery

Earlier I lay down my spinning head on one of the many pillows that infest this place and actually slept for another six hours or so. I didn't even eat first like I had intended, so when I woke up I was ravenous. I do not use that word lightly; I have never felt so hungry. I was dreaming of... (later) Maybe it was my body responding to the shock wearing thin. I tore open another packet of crackers (Crandell's Tea Biscuits—never heard of them, but very dry and oddly satisfying) and opened another jar of the fizzy, tea-colored liquid that passes for water around here (I'd drunk a full one dry in a mad thirst this morning, saying hell with it...)

I stormed out, furious with everything for being so bizarre, and made my way back to the cliffs. It's only about a fifteen-minute stomp from the front door. I had little difficulty, despite the utter lack of any path, in finding the statue again. And of course the sea.

Jesus Christ. The damned, hissing, tea-colored Sea that had shaken me so badly when I first saw it maybe eight hours before. It's like the biggest ginger ale spill in the history of humankind. Except it tastes like mineral water with a hint of soap, if what is in those jars is seawater. No salt. Not salty at all.

I giggled when I wrote the words "ginger ale", as if this were the least bit humorous. This is madness. Let me write it down.

I am 53 years old and I have NEVER heard of a body of water like this on Earth. There are at least SOME insects on Earth. ON EARTH. I'VE GONE COMPLETELY INSANE OR THIS IS NOT EA

I am very very frightened. frightened

i don't know what is real anymore god am i dead?

taking stock --

My name is Avery Alexander Myer. Up until I was twelve I had everyone call me Alex, as I didn't like the name Avery. That was my father's name, too, mhrip—Avery L. Myer. (L? I've always known what his middle name was... why can't I remember now?)

I started keeping a diary at the early age of eight. My father, mhrip, encouraged the practice strongly—hell, he insisted on it. I rebelled in my early teens, as is the wont, but took it up again with a vengeance by 16. There were some gaps during my thankfully brief stint in Vietnam, but I've written at least weekly since then. I find it to be a stabilizing influence. Centering. That's what I am doing now, of course.

My previous diary was lost along with my jacket when

I found a pristine notebook here in the House. It is clothbound, the color of rich mud with tiny green (?) flecks, with hardly any square. The paper is unmarked and bleached a bright white.

I can't remember when I lost my jacket.

I work with books. I repaired them, I read them, and I just noticed I wrote that using the past tense. I repair them. I read them (looks the same). I know what a text block is and why selvedge is used.

My diary writing has become more... loose, emotional, sloppy... in recent years. I think this accurately reflects my mind. I used to be very rigid, disciplined. Especially in my 40's. I never would have written a sentence fragment like that.

I saw a big white bat today. I was numbly wandering the overgrown garden (later) when, just before sunrise, there it was, over my head and flying east. It was huge. It flew like a bird, but it was definitely a bat, or something very bat-like. It was a striking chalk-white, quite like the side of the cliffs. It was tough to judge scale, but I bet its wingspan was at least my arm span.

My back is cramping. There is not a single desk or chair in this place. I shall write more in the garden.

Upon reflection, I might not be dead after all.

But don't quote me.

Aug. 14th, 2004 01:46 am Entry 5

In the garden, (until I couldn't see anymore, then back into the candle light...)

What really gets me about this place is the silence. No birds, no insects and I guess bats don't chirp within hearing range. Yes, plenty more bats, all leaving the cliffs (I'm guessing) and flying overland, their white fur or skin catching the dying light magnificently. Easily two dozen, all moving far less erratically than bats on the hunt. I wonder what they eat.

Silence. A little wind—that's it. When I heard the Sea it was deafening by comparison, though I am sure it's but a whisper compared to city noise. By the House, though, there is a soft whistle of wind and an occasional wooden creak. 24 hours a day. I grew hoarse before I even realized I had been talking loudly to myself.

It occurs to me that this may be one diary that gets found near its writer.

Perhaps I should explain that my parents have since passed away, mtrip, I have one daughter by a woman (Marian) who almost literally vanished from my life two decades ago, and she (my daughter, Robin) has three wonderful grandchildren. I hope they are all right. I hope

I should also explain to anyone who reads this that I have a kind of graphological tic whenever I mention someone whom I loved or respected and has since died, such as my father, mhrip May He Rest In Peace. Now you know.

The thought of someone else reading this is unsettling.

Wow. Sitting ass-deep in a pumpkin patch gone wild and I am covered in little black ants. You don't know how happy I am to see you guys! There are insects after all. I better get inside, anyway, losing light.

I'm filthy, my clothes could walk by themselves, but there is no bath or shower here. I found some sponges and a large bowl by the toilet, so I guess he/she/they had basin baths with seawater.

I've been putting off describing the House, or the statue by the cliffs, I notice. Bad habit of mine; if I don't say it or write it, it really doesn't exist. But they do.

Tomorrow. Tonight, I need a bath.

Aug. 14th, 2004 04:38 pm Entry 6

I dreamt last night.

I was pacing inside the House, my footsteps louder than the whistle of the breeze outside, when I sensed a slight sound from behind the front door. I stopped pacing (in my dream), which served to magnify all the other sounds until I could make out a soft, but sharp hissing. I faced the door, now, for some reason not wanting to approach it. Instead, the sibilance grew in steps, as if something were growing closer—stopping—then moving again. I grabbed onto the irrational certainty that the Sea had come to me since I wouldn't go back to it. The hissing was powerful, the sound seeming unblocked by wood, by the time I realized the water would have had to scale the cliffs to get to the door, but who knows what this place really is and maybe the Sea can pick itself up and rise before you and demand to be let inside...

I woke, my heart thudding away as if I'd run a mile, to the rather soft sound of raindrops on the roof. A few tears slipped down my cheeks and I don't quite know why.

The House has three rooms, plus what looks like an attic that I can't reach. The first room is entered directly from the front (and only) door. The other two rooms are connected by doorways (but no actual doors) to the first room.

The first room is full of pillows of all colors, tall black iron candelabra each holding four candles, a few cotton blankets, a thin wooden stand with a remarkable Go set in mid-game, and a small closet covered by a yellow cloth drape hanging from a rod. I got excited when I first saw that, as I fancied it to be a misplaced shower. No such luck. It is a mostly empty closet with a row of hangers and a few wooden shelves. Of all things, there are four one-piece bathing suits, a magenta bikini and three pairs of men's swim trunks either hanging or stuffed on a shelf. For all that, the space still looks bare and underused.

Could this be somebody's idea of a vacation home?

The second room is where the compost toilet, sponges, towels, magazines and food stores are. This isn't as bad as it sounds, though I was raised to keep food as far away as possible from the bathroom. The food, except for the water and several large boxes of dried fruit, is all kept in a sizable metal locker.

The third room was probably a library at one point, or intended to be, but the 33 shelves are empty except in one corner, where there are some writing and reading utensils (magnifying glass, good quality ball-points, a little battery-operated reading light with no batteries, a rainbow-colored notepad, this notebook). No furniture. Somebody either doesn't believe in chairs or needed them somewhere else.

Outside is the garden I mentioned. It's gone rather wild. I recognize bell pepper plants from my own garden, but most of it is beyond me. The pumpkins, of course. They're the only things producing right now.

I'm packing up some supplies, walking back to the statue and, if I can, to the beach proper. There I will wash my clothes in the Sea and explore.

It's a half-hour later and I'm sitting at the base of the statue.

She (it's hard calling it "it") is almost my standing height, which might make her just shy of six foot. She stands on one leg, attached to a square base mostly covered by the soil. The other leg, her right, is up and out towards the sea, bare toes pointed to where the sun rises, more or less. She's grinning like a child on her first day of summer break, but she looks maybe 20. It's hard to tell, as she is made of... I don't know what she's made of. I'd swear she's solid salt, which prompted me to lick her arm, but no... she's very detailed, down to the denim pattern on her shorts, her individual teeth, the loose fit of her blouse, the zipper on her backpack. The latter is on her back, the straps over her shoulders and held in a hand each. Her salt/stone hair is long and tied into a pony tail. Except for her hips, she's thin as a rail. Enviously, I note her expression is free of all worry.

She's also about to walk off the cliff.

So am I.

Aug. 16th, 2004 05:50 pm Entry 8

The hardest part of walking through the valley of the shadow of Death is the hike back to the car.

I miss my daughter. She has always been the only one to laugh at my jokes, probably because I only started trying to make some after I turned 50. God, I was a humorless bastard.

If there had been any unseen observers during my extended beach camping trip, I would have caught them out, as they would have been howling with laughter. I imagine I provided enormous entertainment, though it did not seem funny to me at the time.

Thinking the statue was placed at that point for a reason, I did my idiot best to climb down the cliff, which was about 60 feet high at that spot. I was enough of a freehand climber to have successfully scaled Devil's Tower in Wyoming on my 27th birthday (actually, one day before). I consider that the pinnacle of my physical development. I was reminded that 27 was many a summer ago.

To my credit, the cliffs here are largely made of this white, sea-bitten, dangerously crumbly stuff that might be chalk. I dropped down my provision bundle (not so smart, either) which snagged on a plant halfway and stayed there. I snarled at the heavens and started my freehand descent.

I had retrieved the bundle and was getting my second wind when my foot mistook a root for a rock and I fell. I hit the dry sand on my back.

The beach exploded.

Sand flew everywhere as THINGS wriggled madly out of the way. I could feel something damn large under me struggling to free itself from my unexpected weight. Even now, writing this in the safety of the House, my skin prickles.

It rapidly became quiet. I lay there face up, hearing the ring of a scream that I belatedly realized was mine. I was terrified, dazed;

an old idiot out of his depth lucky to be alive. The cliffside hid the setting sun, so it was getting dim quickly. I had planned a camp-out, of course, but now I was horrified at the idea of sleeping on the sand. That said, it was a good quarter-hour before I could get up the nerve to even test my limbs. St. Disdo's blessing—I had broken no bones in the fall.

I am as sore as hell now, though. Scared I'm going to lose my back if I keep writing in this position, but I want to get this down while it is fresh.

Walking through the drier sand was doing my heart no favors, as every few feet a foot-long worm would burst from its hiding place faster than a pheasant from a hedge. It was a comfort that they obviously wanted nothing to do with me, but it startled me badly each and every time. So I kept to the wet sand, which was easier, anyway.

It took little time to notice the cliffs were riddled with small caves. Most were well out of reach, but a few were low enough (and big enough) to enter. The weather here had been incredibly mild, but I still wanted shelter, especially considering the hyperactive sand-life. The first cave I entered was dry, clean and bat-free. Making the first prudent decision of the evening,

I unrolled the blanket, ate some figs and crackers and tried to sleep. I awoke before dawn. Soft blue light filled the cave as the sky lightened. I watched quietly as a family of coal-black mice ignored me, cleaning themselves and each other and nibbling on little specks I think were beetles. The cave was only as big as a family car, but they did not seem too concerned when I slowly (not by choice) sat up and went out to scare some worms... that is, relieve my bladder.

God, I'm in pain too sore. Got to tear this place apart looking for aspirin. More later

Aug. 17th, 2004 11:02 pm Entry 9

dream writing in dark

VIVID

In car with grandchildren Anya, Erica, Nathan happy talking about politics w/Anya the eldest

Highway

tires go flat, barely able to control car but I do it

police arrive something is wrong ask me to step out of car

show my license to Officer Pymander I hold it like a playing card

he panics, draws weapon and shoots card makes hole in it

SCREAMING

Aug. 18th, 2004 12:26 am Entry 10

I can't get back to sleep, in so much pain. My handwriting isn't much better than when I was putting my dream down—you should see the position I am in, trying to get some relief from the muscle spasms. Amazing what desperation and a lot of pillows can make.

Damn I am getting old. Could not find a single aspirin. No first aid kits. If they are in the attic it's a shame, as there is nothing to stand on to reach the thing—I managed to push the cover up and over easily enough, but though I can climb a cliff (and fall halfway down) I can not get a good enough grip on the hole to even pull my head up into it. Cut myself trying.

My grandchildren's names are not Anya, Erica and Nathan. I sure as hell would not be talking politics with a six year old. And Officer Pymander? What?

But, and this is the thing, it was SO vivid, like a fever dream or a reaction to total anesthesia—I remember it almost perfectly even now.

Like it really happened to someone.

I wanted to check to see if my driver's license actually had a hole in it, but that disappeared into the ether along with my jacket.

It's a little like I imagine Alzheimer's to be—I can recall my childhood and other distant past memories fine, but I'm extremely hazy on everything that led up to me being here. It scares me. I frankly still haven't ruled out "dead," yet, except I do not think death is supposed to be this painful. Dying, maybe. Death... I hope not.

So. Not much more to tell with the beach exploration, except for the spiders and the chagrin.

After scrubbing my clothes and setting them out to dry, I spent that bright morning looking through the caves I could fit my noggin into, while trying to avoid scaring the caffeinated beach worms (impossible). When I first saw the spiders I immediately thought I was looking at sea crabs. Big BIG white spiders, hiding in some of the moister caves. What is it with the fauna and monochrome? At least the worms are sand-colored, but that is not saying much. Black ants, mice, beetles—white bats, spiders... I saw some long husks by the spiders, so I suspect they eat the worms. The specimens I observed were fist sized for the most part, though there was one that had a grapefruit-sized body and a leg span that I don't want to think about any more. No webs. All the spiders either hunkered down when my shadow passed over them, or outright ran away, which was a relief.

I had my fill of the freakish wildlife by noon, so I decided it was time to get dressed in slightly damp duds and find a break in the cliff wall, as I did not feel good about tackling another 60'.

(I had forgotten my pain, writing this entry, so caught up in remembering... mentioning the 60' reminded me. damn)

I walked and walked and walked, getting stiffer and stiffer, then turned around and walked the other way—and perhaps a half-mile north of the statue, the cliffs sank until they were no more than 10' high.

Ten. Feet.

Howls of laughter from imaginary spies.

As sore as I had become, it STILL took me three tries climbing.

Aug. 18th, 2004 01:13 pm Entry 11

A couple of disturbing things.

I neglected to write down the fact that I went through the tightly stuffed bundle of magazines when I was tired of searching for pain-relievers yesterday. Newsweek, National Geographic, Flaire (never heard of it, some sort of graphic art magazine), a couple of Russian-language mags—none of which were dated later than Jan. 1998.

Disturbing thing #1—A few items were not magazines. One was a thick sheaf of paper solidly stapled three times along the left margin, packed with text. When I first glanced at it

For the merest split-second, I understood it. I could read the sentences, my brain was getting set to interpret the context, then blinding white pain

For a

I can barely write this down. This is so beyond my experience, my understanding of how reality works. For a few very long seconds it felt like someone was inserting a corkscrew just under my left eyeball. My breath caught... I literally couldn't draw air.

It ended, leaving the barest throb which gradually migrated to my temple and disappeared. I was so furious I'm sure I was scared to death but it made me SO ANGRY—I had dropped the paper, but took it right back up and stared at it and DARED it to do that again...!

Nothing. The text was in Latin, which I never studied. I counted the pages: 51, all but the last blank page in Latin. what the hell

Disturbing thing #2—I was paging through a National Geographic article about the city of Tokyo when a hand-torn scrap of paper fluttered out.

See, by this time, I had figured that the statue was placed there just as a reference to find the House. "Walk along the cliffs, find the statue, turn due west and fifteen minutes later there you go." that sort of thing. It made sense.

Too much sense, I'm guessing.

On the scrap was a tiny, beautiful thumbnail pen drawing of the statue. Below that, a matrix of letters that at first I thought was a standard Word Search puzzle, then I thought it might have been a substitution cipher. Not that I can figure. Here it is, triple-checked.

```
V O S N A P T Q M M D S Z L R
G E H M K R P R W K D L V E Z
O B J N T M G P X W S C T X I
E S A K T C P Z W M X F P N R
H A U F C Q L L B G G B X T F
O N W K V I Q B V K R T J W H
I P L G S L A V N Q C P T M S
H E F B T L U X Z Z Q M R H W
```

What is going on here? Is someone playing games? Or did someone really want to conceal a piece of info about the statue for reference later? If so, why?

I'm betting "games," but I am so desperate to find out what is going on, I know I'm going to spend much more time than this crap deserves.

what else do I have to do?

Aug. 19th, 2004 12:14 am Entry 12

When I became tired of beating my head against the letter jumble (definitely not a simple substitution cipher) I did some more exploring, except this time inland.

A light drizzle kept me company. It was nice to taste water that did not have a mineral tang.

I was still within sight of the House's roof when I came across a burned spot on the ground, like some children had lit fireworks a few days before. This was a novelty on the otherwise rolling monotony surrounding me, so I studied it with a strange delight.

The fireworks analogy held; a radiating burn mark on the grass, the main area of which was about the size of a serving platter. There was the impression of a slight crater, or so I thought at first. Two craters, I considered. Or two, somewhat oblong depressions. Then I saw, in the barely damp soil, another depression about 15-16 inches away, southwest from the burn. Then ANOTHER one, a little farther down in the same direction.

And so on.

Footprints.

Wind worn, lightly rained on, but still visible footprints, or, more accurately, shoe-prints. Size 9, I figure.

My size.

I appeared right here. Dazed, in the dark, I was within sight of the House, but stumbled about in the wrong direction for two days before I walked myself into a circle. It took me two days to find shelter that was maybe an eighth of a mile away from zero.

I laughed and laughed until I was on my knees, ripping handfuls of grass in great clods and pressing them into my eyes.

I'm sitting here now, in a nice dry room of the House I'm coming to hate, no longer afraid to say I am going quite mad.

Aug. 20th, 2004 12:10 am Entry 13

Something that is really sticking with me is the look on the cop's face when I hold up my license (in my dream).

He's wearing mirror shades. I present my license as if we were in a cheap magic show --as if to say "is THIS your card, sir?" But he doesn't react like it was the three of diamonds, or even my driver's license. It's like I pointed a pistol at him.

Fear, panic, draw, pow. Hole in the card. By projection, I should think hole in my head, too, although the dream ends there. Perhaps for good reason.

My thoughts are all over the place. I feel like I am evaporating into the thin air of whatever benign Hell I have been assigned to.

Sometimes I imagine I can sense the tubes sprouting from my arms and nostrils, lying as I am in a hospital somewhere with a bullet in my brain. Some cop is anxiously hoping I will pull through so the review board will go easier on him.

Sometimes if I sit very still I can hear the electronic drip of the heart monitor or the pale rasp of the respirator.

I can recall sitting next to Marian as she lay on a hospital bed over-full of instruments, lines and plastic rails. She was so so gray... her lips, her cheeks... like cigarette smoke had become trapped underneath her paper-thin skin.

At other times I embrace this illusion of an alien land, hold it to me like a security blanket. I go outside every day, sometimes twice a day, to watch the beautiful milky-white bats sail overhead. They remind me of seagulls, except with a certain purposeful majesty gulls stubbornly lack.

Then the illusion breaks, eventually... I notice that, all the time I've spent out of doors (nude, even, for hours on the beach while my clothes dried), I never got sunburnt. Or how I walked along that same beach without collapsing in my tracks, despite the fact the Sea bubbles like a soda. Shouldn't I have suffocated if all this CO_2 (or nitrogen or...?) was being produced?

This place is not Earth, it can't be an alien world... either I have been mystically transported to some magical fairyland where physics just does not work the same way... or

or.

Aug. 21st, 2004 04:43 pm Entry 14

So, after a lot of pacing, shouting, notepad tearing, etc. I have solved the letter matrix. For what it is worth. It's getting so these bizarre, metaphysical surprises are just making me sigh and shake my head.

To sum up what was a frustrating, jumbled process—

8 X 15 matrix (= 120 letters)

Only 16 vowels

Exactly two vowels per horizontal line

Half of the vowels appear in the first two positions on each line, and never in both positions on one line.

The vowels, therefor, are markers. The consonants are nothing but placeholders. This took me days to figure out by itself.

15 letters on each line. The 1st two of each line are on/off markers. That leaves one vowel per 13 letter line. Twice 13 = 26. i.e., the number of letters in the alphabet.

The matrix is spelling out eight numbers, one for each line, from 1 - 13 (if there is a vowel as the first letter) and 14-26 (if it is the second letter). Damned inefficient. But not obvious, to put it mildly.

The numbers for each line -

13 +3 = 16
13 + 12 = 25
0 + 13 = 13
0 + 1 = 1
13 + 1 = 14
0 + 4 = 4
0 + 5 = 5
13 + 5 = 18

16th letter = P
25th = Y
13th = M
1st = A
14th = N
4th = D
5th = E
18th = R

PYMANDER

The name of the officer in my dream.

Aug. 23rd, 2004 01:31 pm Entry 15

It has been an eventful couple of days, particularly for a man who has passed on.

About that. I left Entry 13 with an "or" hanging about. After a long while, I came to "or what?" I have trouble describing the tortuous path that went from one to the other. The addition of a "what?" involved more self-reflection, self-pity and gnashing of teeth than I had gone through since my twenties.

If my brain is bubbling creatively away in a stew of oxygen-starved injuries while my flaccid body rots in intensive care somewhere, then nothing here is real except my attitude. I firmly believe that people with a purpose in life live longer and recover faster than those that merely thrash about in the sleep of daily existence. So if I try to survive "here," that can only increase my chances in the world of the salty oceans I love so much.

On the other hand, if where I am is physically real, and most of the time it sure as hell feels that way, then it would behoove me to fight tooth, nail and mind to discover the truth about my situation.

Either way, the process is worthwhile.

Not long after having written my previous entry, I went to the statue to see if I could uncover any detail I had missed. I thoroughly brushed off all the caked soil adhering to the figure's base, which revealed a mostly round, hinged cover lying flush. It was about the size of a half-dollar. I managed to pry it open after some difficulty (I confess with embarrassment my fingernails are all bitten down). Underneath lay a slot the shape of a + sign, perhaps half an inch across. The slot was deep. The cover was obviously there to keep it from filling with dirt.

I am getting the pages of this journal wet, so I will close briefly until I finish my hot tub soak. I will also see if I can find anything to eat in this significantly larger building in which I find myself. I hope I can; my departure was so sudden I failed to take any provisions along!

This is getting serious. I can't find any food in this place, nor can I get back to the House (which I will have to find a new name for).

Looking for the silver lining, at least there are chairs.

As I had earlier gone through every loose item I could find in the House in my search for a medicine kit, I knew that there was nothing that would fit the + like a key in a keyhole.

It was time to do everything I could to get into the attic. At first I was seriously considering the deconstruction of the shelves in the "library" (they were attached solidly to the wall, but...). Then, as I was circumnavigating the House for the nth time, it struck me that a couple of the pumpkins were getting big enough to act as a safer step ladder than stacks of magazines, firmer than cardboard boxes or pillows.

The attic was a warm, dusty space with a ceiling too low to stand properly. Still no medical kit, nor any chairs, but there were tightly bound bundles of the local grass, a few additional food stores, empty boxes and several cartons of biodegradable laundry soap. There was also a card table and a felt-lined box made of brass. It was an anticlimax of sorts (a card table?), but the box was more than interesting. It had five identical spaces, only one of which still had its object ensconced—a key.

It is the most remarkable key I have ever seen. To think there must be four others just like it.

It is as long as a pocket knife, made of a very light metal or ceramic the color of brushed steel. The main body is a fat cylinder with eight rotating wheels. Each wheel has every letter of the English alphabet on it. The rest of the key, the business end, is much thinner, even delicate. It is a smooth cylinder perhaps twice as thick as a pencil lead, clearly designed to rotate and, as I found out by experimentation, with several nested rotating cylinders inside it. The very end has a plus sign cross section about 3/4" long made of eight separate "leaves." These are amazingly thin, even sharp, but strong.

Excited was not the word for it. I risked breaking my neck in the effort to get out of the attic and back over to the statue as fast as I could manage.

I hope I live through that particular mistake.

I spelled out "PYMANDER" on the key, inserted it into the lock, pressed a stud on the large end of the key and BANG.

I am here. Just like that.

Right in front of me had been an old man standing behind a single place setting. Startled my heart into skipping a beat.

Stomach is growling. Going to search again. I wish dinner had been on that place setting.

PLEASE let me find food.

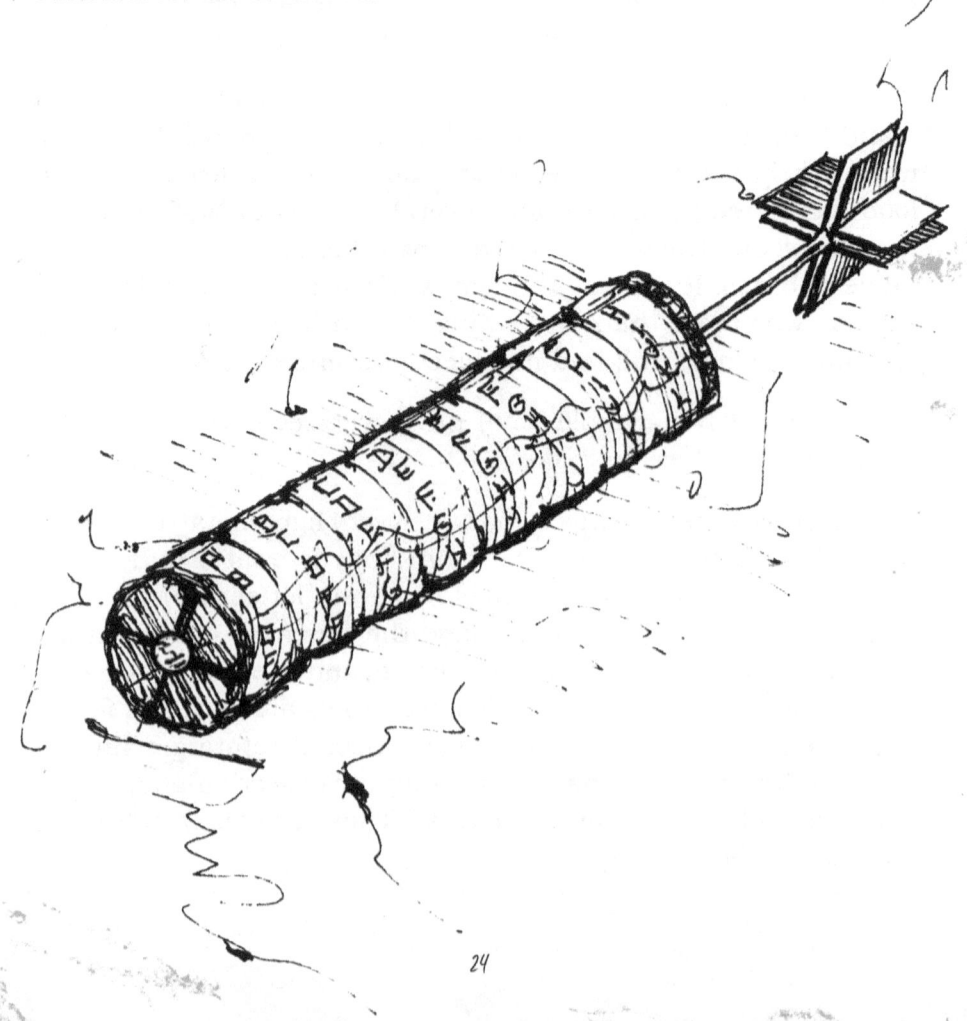

Aug. 25th, 2004 02:53 am Entry 17

An enforced fast is always worse than one I had meant to do, but it's fine. I have achieved, physically, that painless calm that occurs about two days into a fast. It's fine.

My principle goal is to find the combination to the next "area" for lack of a good term. I have found the keyhole here. It was easy; right in front of the mirror, on the floor.

The mirror was the first thing I saw when I burst into this place. I did not recognize my image at first. It was ill-lit, but mostly I was overwhelmed by how much I seem to have changed. I have lost a little weight, my hair looks thinner, I have a beard for the first time since my thirties. My eyes...

So there is a dusty mirror maybe four feet behind a sturdy wooden table. The table was set with a white and gold dinner plate, a tall wooden (and somewhat crude) candlestick (sans candle), a bread knife, and a goblet of the sort one would see at those silly medieval fairs.

Robin sometimes insisted I accompany her to such a fair. I always bitched and moaned, but I always went. I liked the dancing women and the sword fights, I confess.

I find myself in a mansion, compared to the previous vacationer's cabin, with twelve rooms, a bathhouse/basement, and NO EXTERNAL DOORS. I cannot begin to describe how disturbing that is. There are no windows. The only hint of a space outside of the rooms is an occasional lugubrious creaking, as if I were below decks on a dying 18th Century frigate.

Clearly people had once lived here, somehow. I have found, in my search for food and exit, everything from bed-frames to cast iron cookware to a dart board in the pattern of a Mayan calendar. Even found a 1986 Playgirl magazine, for God's sake. There are two toilets, both of a kind I have never seen before in all my travels. Hanging from a thin chain in the ceiling of each bathroom is a book—idle reading, I imagine—one of which is Whitman's "Leaves of Grass," the other contains three of Shakespeare's tragedies. Nothing more delightful than reading "Macbeth" while starving in a windowless prison.

Light just seems to BE, as if it filters down through the fourth dimension. There are no shadows, at all, until the basement, which is nothing BUT shadows. The baths are lit from below by a rich yellow light, serving as the only source. It's both eerie and tranquil at the same time. It's odd that I find it tranquil.

If light isn't an issue to these people, why were there nothing but candles in the beach house? Does each of these places have its own rules? For the love of God, why?

Must rest a little, hand is cramping up.

Aug. 25th, 2004 03:01 am Entry 18

As soon as I finished last entry, thought to look behind the dart board

4

```
O  M  A  C  E  L  C
G  I  R  M  C  N  R
E  A  _  D  _  R  N
H  S  H  E  H  N  S
U  C  _  Z  _  K  E
A  R  D  E  W  E  I
D  I  M  N  H  X  T
```


Son of a bitch.

Aug. 25th, 2004 04:36 pm Entry 19

I have taken to spending most of my time around the baths. The white noise of the water gurgling and dripping provides enormous relief from the nearly dead quiet of, well, everywhere else I have been.

The water here seems wonderfully normal. It is not carbonated or tea-colored. It is not even chlorinated. I think it is continually refreshed through the same system that stirs it around the basins.

My kingdom for a tape player. I was beginning to think these people did not believe in music, until I happened upon the chapel yesterday morning. It's one of the twelve rooms. There obviously used to be pews in the smallish room and, judging from some scrapes on the floor, maybe a piano or organ. All that's there now are a few chairs, two music stands and a sizable stylized sun symbol behind the lectern.

No cobwebs anywhere. No mice or cockroaches. No life. No sign children ever lived here, either.

A part of me can appreciate the sterility, but to live like this?

The steam grays everything out. It's calming, like an eraser is calming. Just removes details, everything can start over.

Feels like floating.

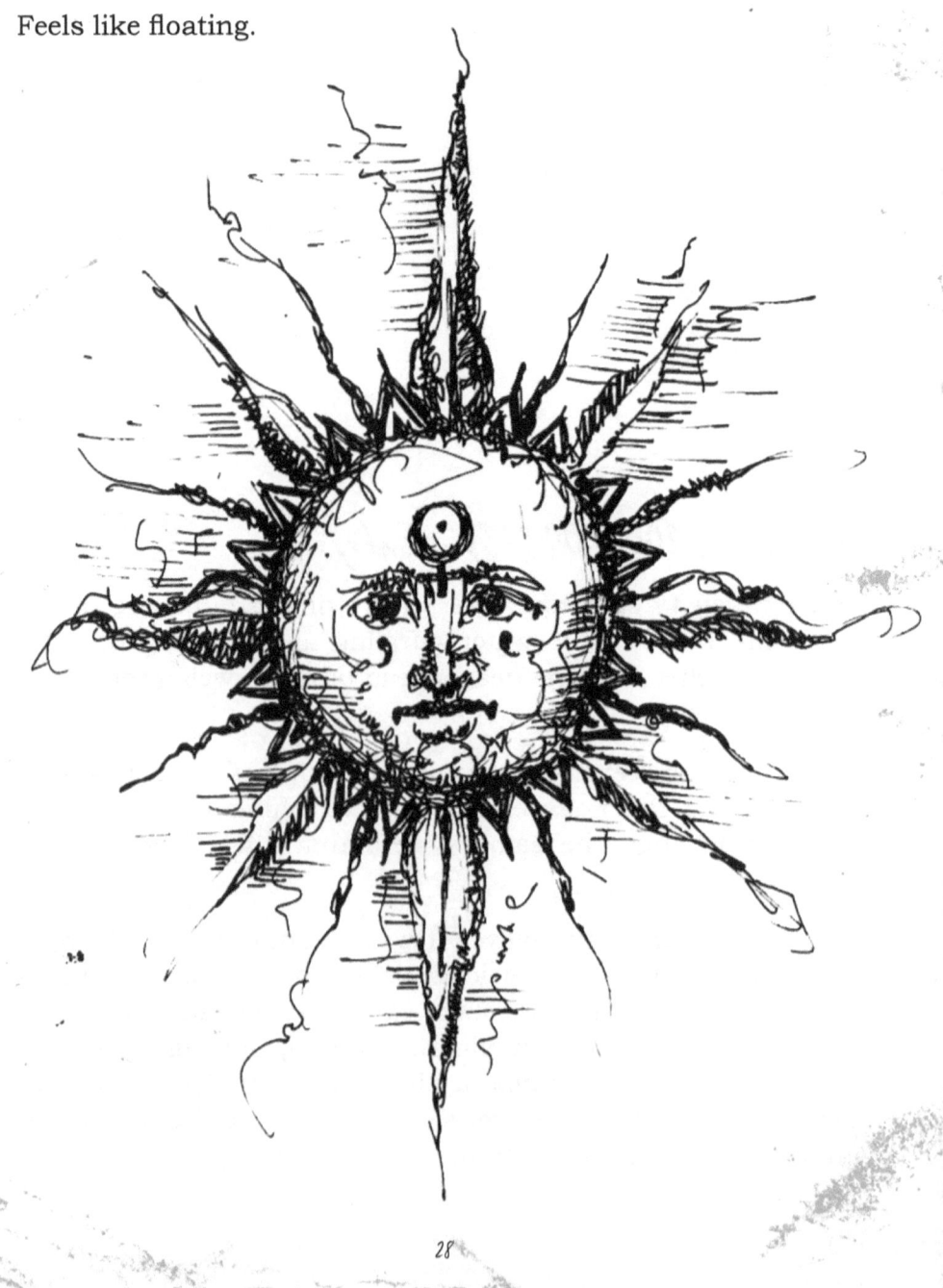

Aug. 27th, 2004 01:42 am Entry 20

"It is not upon you alone the dark patches fall,
The dark threw patches down upon me also;
The best I had done seem'd to me blank and suspicious;
My great thoughts, as I supposed them, were they not in reality
meagre? would not people laugh at me?"
-Walt Whitman, *Leaves of Grass*

My mother, msrip, once made an enormous pie shell as the first
step to a huge Irish meat pie. We had company coming over
that night. I'm having trouble remembering just who, which is
odd, as they were important. It might have been some church
luminaries, or perhaps Masons from the city. Mother, msrip, had
whipped herself into a really wonderful fret, practically skipping
from counter to counter, keeping me close by so I could be on
hand to fetch more potatoes or coal or flour from the cellar. She
also had me chopping like crazy. The pie was supposed to feed
a crowd; she was always of the opinion that quantity impresses
just as much as quality—more so, as it makes the very first
impression.

All the time I was watching her, or chopping vegetables, I had
this numb swelling of dread in my gut, because I knew that
just the day before my father, mhrip, had given away the roast
intended for the pie to a family of Koreans down the block who,
honestly, needed it much more than we did.

I knew this, just as I knew that my mother, msrip, did not. All the
time she was dancing about the kitchen—making sure the stove
was hot enough, rolling the dough, snipping off the appropriate
spices from her windowsill garden—I knew that all Hell would
explode once it became known that the meat had vanished. Yet I
didn't tell her; not so much from a sense of self-preservation, but
from a morbid, even dire curiosity about the coming tempest.

Her reaction went quite beyond anything I had been prepared
for.

When she'd received the news—he looking alternately sheepish and defiantly righteous from the bottom of the cellar stairs—an unhealthy color latched upon her face and visibly crawled down her body. A tremor rocked her gently, as if she had been standing on a train instead of the top of the stairs. I saw her eyes literally sink into their sockets—it is the single most terrible visual memory I have from my childhood. The ladle she had been clutching dropped loudly from her hand, clanging down the cement stairs. Her nerveless body followed it closely.

I sit here in front of the mirror, shaking like a leaf from hunger. I have figured out the puzzle in clear, certain terms. I have the eight letter word which it revealed dialed out on the key. I then placed the key into the hole in front of the mirror and pressed the button.

Nothing happened.

I saw my shocked, colorless face in the mirror inches away and thought of her.

Aug. 27th, 2004 07:40 pm Entry 21

I have been amazed, most of my life, at how readily human beings find patterns. The trait practically forms the backbone of all trade and religious thought. If pressed, I would say that this is because there are patterns to be found.

But not always.

Briefly, (worked up and distracted), I'll explain how I ha ha "solved" the puzzle.

I took the "4" to mean "every fourth letter", so starting from the letter "O" in the upper left corner I counted four to "C", then four more to "R", etc. I continued in the same way on the "inner square" of the matrix until I got eight letters. These letters spelled out CRINAGCK. This is an anagram for CRACKING—as in a code. Get it? It took me a long while and many false starts to figure that out. Oh so clever and oh so wrong.

The "4" might mean "a square" or "four corners" or I don't know. But here it is: start at the "D" in the lower left and go clockwise. Now do the same with the "inner" square corners.

DOCT RINE

"Doctrine." Who are these people?

I have it spelled out on the key. I am sitting here in front of the mirror again. I am looking at the keyhole. I am doing nothing but writing about it in this journal.

Please. Please, whoever you are, please. Let this work. Let there be something to eat wherever it is I'm going and please please let this work.

Aug. 28th, 2004 02:07 am Entry 22

I'm not going to get any sleep until (I hope to God) morning, so now is as good a time as

Jesus.

It's like the gates of Hell have opened out there. It's close to 40 minutes since I wrote "as good a time as" above, as I have had my hands full trying to keep a storm of screaming winged animals (?) from coming inside the shack (Shack). I'm bleeding from several wounds, although none seem to be deep. Fortunately, THIS place has a first aid kit and I should not wonder why.

I materialized

This is not going to work. I can't write while in fear of being torn to piec

Aug. 29th, 2004 04:14 am Entry 23

DOCTRINE worked, obviously.

I have managed a retreat back to the Mansion. The irony is not lost on me, but at least I brought along some food this time. I fully intend to return to the 3rd place (the Swamp), but never again at night. Never.

I have 9 lacerations on my body, all but one superficial. I used a vintage 60's medical kit to sew up the one deep cut just above my hip on the left side. It has been quite a while since I used Mercurochrome. I dearly hope it is still good.

I rescued some MRE's from the Shack. That should hold me for three or four days, but the supply is very limited. As hungry as I am, it has been a struggle to resist eating more than two today.

There's much to write about the Swamp and the Shack and the bloody red sun. But I have slept badly, lost some blood, am barely fed enough... so any more scribbling will wait. I'm just numb. Heaven help me when the shock wears off.

Aug. 29th, 2004 06:02 pm Entry 24

Back in the Swamp. I was sitting and having "lunch" on the landing, but I got weary of the black-flies swarming around my head, so now I am inside this odd little Shack. In a half-hour I will take the skiff over to the landing again, there to retreat to the 2nd place before sundown.

I really have to work out a nomenclature for these bizarre places.

The shock has worn off and, as a pleasant surprise, I seem to be fairly stable. My side hurts like a bitch, but there is no sign of infection, yet, so things are looking cautiously up.

All right. Backing up. When I first materialized, it was on a wooden landing built over the water of the Swamp. My ears popped. The smell and chewy humidity of the air were overwhelming after the disused sterility of the Mansion. The atmosphere ripples with the noise of enormous blurs of insects. Amazing, tall bald cypress are everywhere, most covered in some sort of parasitic vine. The water, I have since been able to tell, is usually around four feet deep. I had to test that with a pole, as the water is murky. Or possibly it is the light.

The sun is dim and bloody. Besides being eerie, it screws up color perception. The water might be fairly clear, but the light is so bad that anything green appears black.

The landing: it's attached to nothing, built over the water upon pilings. It's made of what looks like highly treated 2 X 4's. Next to the landing is a step. Tied to the step, fortunately, was (and is) a skiff.

Time has passed, I'm back at the landing.

On the landing is a statue. A female, again, the representation this time is in lacquered wood. She's life-sized, just like the last one. She appears African and is more zaftig than the white-stone sculpture. She is sitting on the landing with her bare feet just above the water. A kind of headdress is draped artfully, concealing her hair and framing her full face. Her cheeks show a kind of ritual scarification. She wears a one piece dress or pareo that covers her well from just above her full breasts down to maybe six inches below her knees (which are crossed). She's leaning back slightly and resting on one hand behind her. Across her lap is a short staff or rod (still wood and all part of the statue) while her other hand holds a (wooden) cut flower (not quite a rose—not sure what it is supposed to be). There is a quiet, even regal dignity about her, but also a wistfulness to her expression. She is looking off to the southwest.

Speaking of the west, what passes for the Sun here is getting dangerously close to the horizon. I probably have another hour, but better safe than ripped to ribbons. The Shack, next entry.

Aug. 31st, 2004 03:11 am Entry 25

Spent the day carefully exploring the area. Managed not to get too lost.

Drifting quietly on the skiff, only occasionally ducking a branch or spider-web—it threatened to become a profound experience. My dreams have been broken and incomplete this last week, except for a few vague but intense ones concerning food. I have come to the tentative conclusion that my dream about getting stopped on the road (by Officer "Pymander") is an embellished version of actual events, either leading up to my appearance here or actually causing it, somehow. This makes little sense, of course, but then what has, lately. I feel it strongly, though. They feel like memories.

The Shack is a wooden affair built tall on pilings, maybe five feet above the water. A tiny landing—much smaller than the one with the statue—is just big enough to park the skiff. A well-made staircase then leads to a catwalk that takes you to the front (and only) door. These people do not believe in emergency exits, when they believe in exits at all.

Inside are two rooms, close and stuffy, smelling of mildew, coal smoke and something else I can't identify. There are two windows with stiff screens. Ten replacement screens are stacked near the door.

It used to be eleven, but during the harrowing night I spent in there, one of the screens was breached by the sharp screeching nightmare things. No more have been damaged since, so maybe they had been trying extra hard to get fresh meat. I don't know.

Two fluorescent lanterns hang from the ceiling by a couple links of chain. I presume they are battery operated. They were off when I arrived and they both work just fine.

Which again begs the question: why this inconsistency with light? Candles, sourceless illumination, what looks like military issue lanterns—it's all such a weird, hyper-eclectic patchwork. Everything is. Not just the lights.

"Military issue" is indeed a theme, in the Shack. There are four cots, a box with Meals Ready to Eat (rapidly disappearing), a cabinet with the medical kit and a military canister of insect repellant, and four clean Mossberg 500 military shotguns with kits and several boxes of shells. I take one of these weapons along during trips from the Shack, but so far it has been completely unnecessary. I do not see any walls blown apart, so no one has been firing them inside, which was a serious temptation when several of those razor bat whatever creatures threatened.

But there are some decidedly nonmilitary things, too. A gold lamé privacy screen so you can crap into the glorified bucket/honeypot in peace; a small coal-burning stove complete with tongs and a little coal tote (why? it is very warm here... it must get chilly at some time... or maybe just to boil water?); a tackle box; and some bottles of a lethal, homemade, sweet alcoholic beverage that came in very handy when I was sewing myself up, as there is only aspirin in the medical kit. Extremely high proof, quite devastating, almost like Everclear someone had added herbal tea and honey to.

I have to import my drinking water from the Mansion.

One more strange thing before I close for the night: as I was paddling about in the skiff (it has both oars and a pole), I wandered to the back of the Shack and saw what might be a clue to the next eight-letter puzzle. Extending out from the back wall, perhaps nine or ten feet above the water, are eight wooden additions that look like square upside-down "U" shapes. They are all lined up horizontally. The shapes, appearing like six inch chutes angling slightly downwards, do not otherwise seem to have any purpose. It's only that fact, plus the number, that compels me to write it down in here.

Otherwise, I have found no evidence of another puzzle.

I had better learn to fish.

Aug. 31st, 2004 02:25 pm Entry 26

I'm furious without knowing who to be mad at. This whole setup is a game, but one which will end with me in a pool of blood at the bottom of a skiff.

Shortly after dawn, I materialized back to the Swamp. I wanted to explore the area in the opposite direction as yesterday. As usual, I started at the Shack as point zero.

As I passed the back wall, I was slightly startled to see a dim flash of green out of the corner of my eye. This was remarkable because in this strange sunlight green looks black. I glanced up at the eight wooden constructions I wrote about earlier, which were little more than dim outlines in the post-dawn light. It took a minute of squinting and focus shifting to make out an extremely faint green glow coming from each bracket.

I am pretty sure the fourth one is an "H".

I probably sat there, mouth catching flies, for

When I find who made this

The clue can only be read AT NIGHT.

Sep. 2nd, 2004 12:28 am Entry 27

It is far too easy to get drunk on the beverages here.

The stuff makes for good lighter fluid, also.

After a night of little sleep in the Mansion, I'm spending a harrowing night of zero sleep in the Shack. The night is screeching black bloody revenge outside walls that suddenly seem all too thin. I'm writing by the scant light of a coal fire in the stove, sweating like my football coach in high school, in the theory that leaving the lanterns off would not attract the flying things so much. At first, that seemed wrong. Now, though, it does sound like they are a bit thinner outside—that, or I am just getting used to the cacophony. The new screens are holding, knock on hopefully solid wood.

The keepers of the Shack, whomever they may be, had the quirky foresight to place a brass lighter inside the stove which I thought was actually a great idea, although that's probably both the booze and the relief talking. If I had known where all this was going, I'd have saved some matches from the 1st place. Hell, I'm not sure I would have left the 1st place.

So I splashed a little of the current bottle onto the few lumps of coal inside the stove, leaned in, flicked the lighter (first try!) and whoomp, nearly singed my eyebrows off. But the stove is lit, hooray. I can sit here, burning hot, writing about how my side aches every time one of those horrible things slaps into the wall, which is a lot.

Actually, not so often, now. That's nice.

later: you know, not often at all. what the hell. I just looked out the screen and the night is still black with those goddam creatures, but theyre staying the hell away from the place

thats funny

man Im drunk

Sep. 2nd, 2004 05:10 pm Entry 28

Tonight is the night.

My hangover this morning was dreadful, but not as bad as I had feared (deserved). Drunk as I was, I had managed to switch back on the lanterns in an attempt to see if the darkness was keeping the creatures away. There was no great effect that I could tell.

It was the stove. Rather, it was the smoke spewing out of the vent pipe that rose from the stove through the ceiling. It did not seem to keep them away very far, or perfectly. But I feel nearly certain it is the solution. If not, I could pour a bottle of the herbal moonshine onto the water and light it; watching the entire Shack go up in flames would be briefly satisfying. Since I have eaten the last of the MRE's this afternoon, though, it would be a bad idea.

Here is the plan: light the stove, throw in some damp grasses for extra smoke, get out on the water and try to make out the eight letters. Assuming I am not flayed alive, get back into the Shack, rest up, out to the landing and use the key, which will hopefully teleport me inside a Ritz-Carlton and not smack into a Hellhole worse than this one.

I can dream.

Sep. 4th, 2004 12:19 am Entry 29

You know that feeling when you see or hear something so familiar that for an instant you know precisely where you have experienced it before, but after a scant moment the identity fades, leaving only the aggravating sense of familiarity? And no matter how hard you smack your head or rant at your faulty brain, nothing will bring that miniscule passage of clarity back?

It adds a whole new dimension when you do not know if your life depends on the answer, or not.

I appear to be back at the Seltzer Sea, as I've chosen to name this place. However, if that is true I must be some distance away from the House. I still find myself next to the water, on the beach. Rather, in a nicely dressed cave inside the cliffs. But the cliffs here are much taller—close to 200 feet I figure. The beach is facing south, not east. There is a greater variety of vegetation, probably because of a stream that has cut its merry way into the cliffs, flowing through the beach and into the Sea.

There is another statue.

The cave is equipped with a wooden door not unlike the one to the House. Inside it is clear that, as usual, most of the furnishings and personal belongings have been cleared away, as if these places were converted from an eccentric, collective living space to

I do not know how to finish that sentence. To what, a giant brain teaser? It seems TOO cluttered for that. What were the shotguns for? Why four of them? Did the creatures in the Swamp erupt out of the water at night JUST to provide an obstacle for reading the clue? Or was the clue fashioned so as to take advantage of the murderous nightlife because, gosh darn, a letter matrix just does not involve enough blood and misery?

The word was "ALCHEMIC," by the way.

Is this place an emergency crash-pad, once used to entertain dignitaries, but now left disused unless some idiot gets popped with a police-issue

I can't finish that sentence, either. I simply do not want to return there.

Which leaves me in this sparse, but somewhat pleasant den, eating a granola bar, drinking a warm and way too old bottle of Coors Light (I assume... it could be extremely stale sea water... flavored with hops...) in pitch blackness relieved only by four of the same sort of candles as found in the House. By day, the two rooms are lit by some sort of system that pipes sunlight. I will need to investigate that further.

Besides the food, the thing that has caught my intense interest (and was responsible for the first paragraph) is a painting hanging on the wall. It shows what at first looks like a scene from a witch trial: hapless (but defiant) woman in a plain dress tied to a stake, the timbers below her feet just starting to show the flames. Facing her are undoubtedly her accusers, probably the judge(s) and constabulary. All are male, although several are decidedly androgynous, oddly. Also oddly, closer examination reveals the accusers all are equipped with modern sidearms. They are not elated by the execution, but are just as dead serious, even defiant, as the victim.

The whole thing is in a simple, quality wooden frame. A brass plate under the frame says "The Crime". And, yes, I noticed that makes eight letters and, yes, I tried that out on the key by the new statue. Nothing. Could not be that easy, could it.

The thing about the painting, for me, is the woman.

I have seen her before. I have known her—known her, spoken with her (just about hear her voice), fought with her, cared about her. I am sure of it. SURE of it.

But for my life, I don't know who she is.

Sep. 5th, 2004 06:03 pm Entry 30

Things I should have been thankful for: music, hot and cold running water, someone to talk to, a closet full of clean clothes, cold beer, my granddaughter's laugh (starting up very high and moving down the scale), the way my daughter's nose wrinkles when she frowns, Omar's Grocery just around the corner, my astrolabe, watching my grandchildren play (whether it was Candy Land or Checkers or just running around as children do), making bread

If I squint, I can just make out an island off shore.

Last night, I dreamt I could walk to the island, over the water, but as I did so, it never grew closer. After a while I lost sight of the mainland; I knew with a dream's certainty that it was gone and I could not go back, nor would I ever reach the island. There I was, standing on the surface of a perpetually hissing Sea, knowing I would sink if I slept, but I had nowhere to go.

I woke wondering if I had fallen asleep.

Sep. 7th, 2004 03:32 am Entry 31

I have been taking advantage of the unrelenting peace and quiet here by catching up on some much needed sleep. At my age this becomes a blessed thing. I had been running myself so literally ragged that I have been on the brink of collapse for a while, now. My side is beginning to itch, hopefully indicating the healing process is progressing. I hate to write this, but the sutures will probably need to come out in a couple of weeks or so. Something to look forward to.

As my mind fractures, it is distantly interesting to witness all the myriad complications as they blossom and fade.

God, that is a dark, baroque sentence. I struggle with keeping my thoughts evenly divided between observation and introspection, but more and more I find myself regressing to my teens and twenties—full of circular thoughts, angst, isolation. This time, of course, the isolation is extremely real. I am on a desert island, with each passing ship dropping me off to another damn island.

There is a pretty good store of nonperishable foods here. This time I will create a little bundle of provisions in case I wind up stuck and starving again. I imagine I will grow very weary of (taking account) granola bars, potted meat, soda crackers, dried apricots and pears, two tins of kippers and one cute little jar of Vegemite. I should not lack for salt, anyway. But food, I have rediscovered, is food. I count my blessings, even if the bottled beer has gone bad.

Not that I seem to be going anywhere; no clues, at all. Well, who knows: there's another (rather sad) collection of limp magazines stashed inside the outhouse (forgot to mention that --about 30 feet from the statue, nicely built from wood), but no pieces of paper conveniently falling to the floor this time. Reader's Digest (in both English and Cyrillic alphabets), one National Geographic (Sept. '93), an issue of The Rotarian, and a paperback of Peanuts cartoons. The latter provided more comfort than I can easily admit.

So who knows. I have tried about twenty near-random wild guesses with the key so far, with predictable results. My eye keeps getting irresistibly drawn to the victim in the painting I described, but as I don't recall who she is, I certainly hope the key's answer is not her name. I will be here a long time indeed.

Okay, I have been dragging my metaphorical feet about the new statue, probably because I find these the most affecting, frustrating part of my whole experience.

Plain observations: it is another woman, carved out of the same bright white stone as the 1st one, again in marvelous detail. She is kneeling upon an elevated, earthen rise, so her knees are about chest level to me. They are covered in a long skirt, which is her only apparel save for a fairly heavy glove on her right hand and a large hair clip keeping her long, straight hair out of her way. She is wearing the glove, I imagine, to provide a grip for the sizable, ornamental sword she has a hold of (point down into the earth, her hand on the grip). A smallish, badge-shaped shield is leaning on her opposite hip, as if removed from her left arm and resting on the ground. She might have done this because she needed her left hand for—this is going to read like complete kitsch, but actually it looks soft and serene in context --for gently lifting her breast, from which flows an actual stream of water. Her face has a bit of Classical Greek about it. Her gaze is lightly bemused, flawed by a slightly furrowed brow, as in concentration or distant concern. Her attention is directed at the stream of water. She has what are probably supposed to be thin scars around her collarbone and one on her right cheek, so she has seen some combat. Not lately, I trust, despite being armed, for she is obviously far into pregnancy; her belly is stretched round and extends naked above her skirt. Even her white stone naval has popped out.

The "milk" is probably supplied by the stream racing down the narrow ravine. It tastes yes I have tasted it like a lighter, less bubbly version of the Sea, for which I am grateful.

All women, except for the 2nd place where there was no statue at all. This all must mean something. Who would create such amazing works of life-sized art for no reason. Hell, there are not even any tool marks on these things.

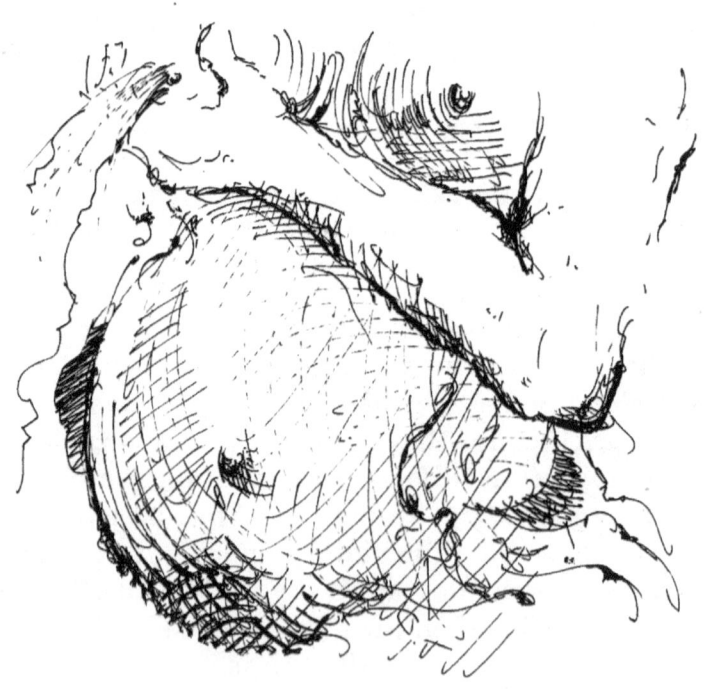

Sep. 7th, 2004 05:37 pm Entry 32

"I can't be certain, but I think they saw me."

I was dozing in front of the painting entitled "The Crime", drifting here and there amid a jumble of images behind my eyelids, when I heard with crystal clarity a woman say the above sentence. I was startled just enough into wakefulness that I entered that weird stage where I am aware of my surroundings, but can neither open my eyes nor move my limbs. It only lasted a few seconds, until the rest of my brain caught up and I woke fully, but during that brief time I wrestled with consciousness, trying hard to catch who might be in the room with me.

In retrospect it was pretty irrational. I have had minor auditory hallucinations before, once in a great while, when I am halfway asleep. This was one of them. But I wonder. Did I hear the woman in the painting? Did she say that to me, once? That really unnerves me.

There was real fear in that voice.

Sep. 8th, 2004 11:08 pm Entry 33

I was walking along the beach today, heading west, marveling at how used to the hyperactive sandlife I have become, when I happened to come across another ground-level cave entrance in the cliff wall. Eager to explore more than the shore, I gave it a peek. The opening appeared relatively recent, as if it had been knocked away by human hands, rather than eroded. Inside was no bigger than 15 feet square. Moderately dry, it had managed to preserve the one thing that had been left there, probably several years ago.

A used condom, now brittle and shrunken, like a dried earthworm.

I laughed and laughed. I was not sure why at the time, but now, having reflected, I think I was deeply relieved to see some evidence that the people involved in my predicament, however intimately or obliquely, were indeed human beings, after all.

I searched the place for more evidence of habitation (or fornication), mind wandering, thinking how this cave had once been a hermetically sealed bubble of white rock. It was not until I was walking back to the Cave (the furnished one) that my mind started piecing together various bits of information.

I literally stopped so abruptly that I fell to my knees. For the second time, I laughed. I bet they heard me all the way to that island to the south.

The answer to the next puzzle HAD been right in front of me, after all. It might not have been as easy as reading it, but almost...

"The Crime"

"hermeTiC"

I have not checked it yet, but how can that not be right. I better make sure I am packed, yes?

Sep. 10th, 2004 02:51 am Entry 34

Good news: it worked. Beginning to see a theme with these clues.

Bad news: I am fairly sure it took me back to the dim red sun place, although not the Swamp, thank the Lord. I am heading back to the Cave to recover my nerves and write much more down. I will explain, but right now I must copy something that might be important.

You lead me by the hand
into the golden Great Hall,
taking no pity on my bare
bruised feet, out past the
Courtyard Major where,
like God's very breath,
mists
tickle
every fright and fancy
my poor mundane mind
can conjure. You spin

the Wheel and call a
Name—Seven of the
Eight respond, and we
proceed into the Light.

I am starting to get a feel for where a clue will show. I think this might be it.

I would stay and write more, but something is moving just behind the only door to this horror show and I simply refuse to bait Hell.

Sep. 10th, 2004 11:53 pm Entry 35

I have been reluctant to revisit the 5th place. I suspect if I have any hope of returning to what I believe was my life, I need always to go forward, but

It is so peaceful here. My motivation flags; it seeps like liquid into the sand. When I had arrived, however that happened, at the House, my shock and disbelief kept me searching. When the shock wore off, it was the need for food that fired me. Now that I have a fair stock of food, for the time being, I can sense a great languidness, a lassitude, hold me to this barren, incomplete, abandoned place.

No not peace, not acceptance.

Fear.

Damn it all. I am becoming a coward. I am (must admit) terrified of what is around the next corner.

Now that I have experienced the 5th place (the Guard Post?), it has become increasingly apparent that my captors/testers, the people who moved and left the clues to navigating this nightmare, it has become clear that they found this place. They did not create it. They found it and modified it to their own needs, but there were some things they could not deal with, or control. I was just beginning to think that I was being lead from place to place, perhaps scaring me, but never actually putting me in a situation I could not get myself out of. I mean, is it coincidence that each of these puzzles has been something I can handle? I like to think I am an intelligent man, but all they had to do was make one of the anagrams a Russian word and I would be sunk. Or a letter matrix with null characters. They deliberately set out to create puzzles that did not need a code key or a book to solve. Why?

But now, it has settled into my brain that the next place I teleport to might be obliterated, or under water, or ransacked. The clue might be destroyed, moved, altered...

As I wrote before, the 5th place is a part of the same world in which the Swamp exists. That's my theory, anyway. The statue is made of the same material as the zaftig one at the Swamp. Both of the statues at the Seltzer Sea are similar to each other, too, so I wonder if the materials represent the land. Plus, the atmosphere seems to share a few characteristics, despite being in a climate controlled complex.

However, I could not see the sun, red or otherwise. The Guard Post is a single room the size of a four-car garage. The only exit is a metal and ceramic? door literally melted shut. What I presume is a small square glass window on the door has been thoroughly taped over with duct tape and brown paper. There are no windows in the room, otherwise. Instead, there are several audibly blowing air vents close to the ceiling, two banks of nine TV monitors each (several are inactive, a few obviously ruined and leaning precariously out of their housing), a control station for the monitors, two lab tables that have been converted to what are hopefully hospital beds, several IV stands, an eyewash station, three big and extremely locked steel cabinets, black and white checkerboard tile on the floor, fluorescent lighting above, and the aforementioned statue.

What had kept me there for hours, as well as eventually chasing me away, were the monitors. They could be switched from location to location and, more often than not, a little joystick would pan each camera position. What I saw in my virtual explorations gave me deep, visceral chills.

Getting woozy. I have been putting off sleep for long enough. I confess I am worried about nightmares. Some of those images have wormed their way into the holes of my brain.

Sep. 12th, 2004 12:58 am Entry 36

One of my theories for these statues has been blown to pieces, as this one is a male.

He is a big guy: sizable arms, thick legs, solid jaw. He would be at least as tall as I if he stood on his feet, but he sits on a stump with his knees perhaps a foot apart and his hands clasped tightly together, elbows on legs. His brow is heavy and serious, his hair thinning in front, but long and a little wild. A simple, thin crown rests slightly askew on his head. His expression falls just short of "angry." More like impatient mixed with deeply troubled. What I presume is a thick animal fur (does not translate perfectly to polished wood) is draped over his shoulders and back. The artist did a magnificent job at giving the fur an appearance of weight. His breeches are primitive, but sturdy, with several skin or maybe cloth ties. Massive, shaggy boots are on his feet. A sheathed sword (all wood) rests in back of and leaning on the stump. He is not handsome by any stretch, although he radiates a cruel (and maybe cunning) authority.

If a title at the bottom had said "Conan" I would have accepted that. Not that he resembles the Governor of California.

Lastly, around his neck is a large necklace that is NOT part of the statue, i.e. it is a real necklace. It seems to be made of rectangular black glass chunks alternating with much smaller round gold beads. It's quite the clan-chieftain style. I started to pick it up on my first visit, but by that time I was so disturbed by the images on the monitors that—not sure how to describe this—I found it hard to approach the statue too closely. It is quite realistic, as they all are, and moving up close enough to touch the jewelry gave me the literal shakes, as if my sense of self-preservation had kicked in for no rational reason. Prickles of sweat oh enough enough

I have a cloud behind my eyes.

Not sure what that means, but it is true.

Sep. 13th, 2004 01:29 am Entry 37

I am taking a break from trying to wrestle some meaning out of that "poem" I recorded two or so days ago, so I can put down a disturbing image from a dream last night.

In my dream, I actually did pick up the necklace from around the statue. When I touched it I got a tangible sensation of vacuum, as well as a weird synesthesian sound of ice cracking. I suddenly became aware of a presence behind me. I left the necklace on the wooden neck and turned.

Myself. Thinner, with more hair, yet not younger. Oddly jointed; bent. Tight, constricting bands of cloth-like metal around both the eyes and the mouth, rendering him/it/me blind and mute. It stood without a full weight, as if it were being suspended from a single, unseen line, letting only its toes touch the floor. It shimmered very slightly, as if behind a slightly uneven pane of clear glass. And it was me.

I woke up overwhelmed. Reality seemed to oscillate above the futon where I lay. My vision swam with tiny particles. For a brief second I thought I might still be dreaming, but I blinked and everything snapped back to clarity.

Back to the verse—it looks like contrived, vaguely Masonic drivel. My father, mhrip, was more than a little suspicious of Masons. His father (my grandfather, mhrip) was a Shriner, which I was told was essentially "a drunk Mason." Such a dry wit.

Initial letters are not revealing anything earth shattering. The number of words or letters in a line might be significant, but despite hours trying different permutations I can not see how.

Capitalized words are probably involved, but again... What the Hell was that dream about? Was it just underlining my powerlessness, here?

Just like this place, there are too many strange details in that dream that do not add up, as if there were a dozen layers of meaning, or an enormous "big picture" of which I know zero, or (just as disturbing) that so much of my circumstance is arbitrary—just like life—but how could this place be REAL?

Am I searching so hard for answers I would be horrified to know?

Sep. 13th, 2004 05:24 pm Entry 38

It is a good thing I talk to myself like a doddering old man, or I might not have ever figured out this latest puzzle. I am still shaking my head. Oh, yes, I will have a word or two with whoever wrote this, yes sir.

Say the seventh and eighth lines out loud. There's the answer.

I dialed that on the key, offered it near Conan's stump and got the heck outta Dodge. And into a church on top of a mountain. It is COLD in here. I will write more once I get my hands warmed.

What sort of church needs a cage?

I can skip places.

I just assumed one had to proceed sequentially, perhaps because I had been forced to that mode going forward. Then, well on my way to developing hypothermia but not wishing to visit the disturbing Guard Post, I dialed in for the Cave and it worked. Not knowing the word for the 1st place I still can not return there, but everywhere else is open. As small as this victory is, I find it liberating.

Like a trapped animal discovering its pen is bigger than it thought, I suppose.

I have commandeered some sheets and a blanket from the Cave in order to bear the low temperatures of the 6th place.

The Church sits atop a tall mountain (my ears popped something fierce) of orange-gray rock barren of life, except for sparse tufts of prickly grass, small birds, cricket-like things, lichen, and twice now I have seen larger, oddly shaped creatures flying a long distance off. It is cold, it is extremely dry and the air is markedly thinner than I am used to. The sky is such a light blue it is almost white. The view is magnificent. The sky has been cloudless up above, but down below the mists collect in patchy white piles, occasionally revealing the sharp green of a lush valley many miles away. The air smells of dust, but is visually crystal clear. The breeze is surprisingly light, thanks to God, for the chill would be unbearable. The sun is as bright as an ice field and seems just as warm. The nights so far are too cold for me to take for long, dressed as I am in what are rapidly becoming rags.

The Church is the size of a small town church, with seating for perhaps 120. It is airy inside, though the numerous windows are small and uncolored. The heavy wood is cracked and dry like a shoreman's skin. The ceiling is peaked, with a minimum of crossbeams.

On one wall are inch-high blue letters about head height; they read "And their prayer, if offered in faith, will heal him, for the Lord will make him well; and if his sickness was caused by some sin, the Lord will forgive him."

Now to the weird stuff: there is the statue, of course... Another male, it is made of the same tawny stone as the mountain, except for a plain tall staff he "holds" in one hand—it is made from a light wood. He looks like he belongs here. That is, he is pretty clearly a church authority of some kind. He is in the classic right-hand-up-palm-out pose, the left hand curled possessively around the staff. He is starkly handsome, but serious. Robes seem to drape him. His head is bereft of hat and his hair is cut mostly short (it's perhaps a little too long in back to be a modern Protestant pastor). He looks somewhat Nordic.

Right next to him is the pulpit. It is a normal pulpit, made of a particularly dark wood. The only odd thing is a hole drilled into the floor about two feet in front of it. I suspect something... maybe the staff... was meant to go there for some reason.

It might have something to do with the beam of light, or perhaps the cage. But I am yawning every ten seconds, now, and my eyes are watering. Time to retire (in the comfort of the Cave).

I must find new clothes.

Sep. 17th, 2004 02:41 am Entry 40

17¢

That's how much cash survived my translation into this madhouse.

I find that the coins have less reality to them. I do not mean that they are actually fainter or lighter, but when you remove the entirely mental quality of "money", they are nothing but tiny disks of cheap pressed metal. I have a dime, a nickel and two pennies, and at no time has anything seemed less useful or natural.

I found an outhouse nestled in a wide crevice perhaps 200 yards away from the Church. I was beginning to wonder. This has led to another mini-crisis, though (one that does not often make it into a Grisham thriller)—toilet paper. I am glad someone had already removed the Bibles from the church. That neatly sidestepped a little moral quandary...

I have gone through the Cave's meager supply already, which meant that I had to pop over to the Mansion to pick up some more. The House (the 1st place) was well stocked indeed, but once again I can not get there. And I absolutely refuse to use the stiff, white paper of this journal for that purpose.

To think I was starving mere weeks ago.

Which is another thing—no food here. No much of anything. Except the weird stuff. Finish the description.

Every realm here seems to have its disturbing feature. The cage is that feature in the Church. Situated in the chancel with the short end against the wall, the cage is about three feet wide and high, between five and six feet long. There is a closed, hinged door with a simple drop latch. It is not locked, so it would be easy to open and crawl into. Why would I want to do that? Because the end against the wooden wall is devoid of bars, i.e. there is no cage wall, it shares the wooden wall. On the wooden wall is a wooden box, of the kind used to donate money to the poor, except the slot of this one has been sealed over with something (plastic? putty?). It is also firmly latched.

This is a test, of course.

I need to open the cage door, climb inside and unlatch the box, which undoubtedly reveals the next eight letter answer (or something equally important). What is stopping me from doing just that is the rubbery Hellspawn creature also in the cage.

I kid not. When I first saw it, I thought it was a black rubber medicine ball or badly melted tire. It was (and still is) directly illuminated by an angled beam of light, originating from the ceiling of the nave from what looks like a recessed lighting fixture in the middle, but it probably isn't a conventional spot lamp since there is no electricity that I can tell. It is bright blue, landing smack on the big black ball. In the spirit of experimentation that I have developed in order to survive here, one of the things I did was block the light by partially draping the cage with a blanket. As soon as that happened, the "ball" whipped instantly to life, as if I had thrown a 50,000 volt switch. It went ballistic.

I can write about this calmly now, but at the time I literally wet myself. The thing was LOUD, it was insanely frenetic and it was horrifying to watch. Black tendrils, each flashing with numerous short teeth, exploded from the thing as it bounced violently around like a hornet in a cup. All its action eventually (it was probably only seconds) knocked the blanket off of the cage; the light hit it and the thing collapsed in on itself instantly. Frozen, motionless. A melted black rubber ball.

I stood and stared for a minute, no exaggeration. Then, thinking in the manner to which I am becoming accustomed (or trained), it began to dawn on me just what had been demonstrated.

I need to get past the demon to open the box in order to progress. How appropriate.

I have shamed myself into ignoring this diary for the last few days.

I have become the model of overpreparation. I retrieved one of the shotguns from the Shack and have been wasting precious ammunition practicing with it. I have pulled the stitches from my side wound. I went through every permutation of the Bible quote I could think of to see if it contained the eight-letter answer. I have gone back to the Mansion to see if, illogically, there were anything I missed that could be a clue. I've done everything I could think of to avoid the inevitable, except learn to juggle.

I would even write in this journal to confirm once more that I am not as brave as I would like to be.

I keep telling myself that the creators of these tests did not seem to have the destruction of the quester in mind, yet I think back to the Shack and what a messy call that was. How deadly that came close to becoming. And I think back to the tightly sealed Mansion and how I might have starved to death. Then I look at the cage. I have waking dreams of the thing inside tearing me into a million thumb-sized shreds.

I have long since removed the staff from the statue and set it into the hole in front of the pulpit. The staff fits pretty well. The top of it just barely falls short of the light beam, leading me to guess that there is something no longer around that used to crown the staff. How very Indiana Jones.

So what am I going to do.

I screwed up the courage to poke and prod the inert Hellbeast. It truly comes across as utterly unliving, so long as the light is upon it. I have been sorely tempted to shoot it point blank through the cage, but somehow I just know that will only make it mad...

I am going to open the cage, block the light, ready the shotgun and try not to fire so wildly that I obliterate my own feet. I should also leave the doors open so it will have an escape route.

That's what I am going to do.

But first, learn to juggle.

Sep. 23rd, 2004 08:06 am Entry 42

I get the lesson. I think.

Exactly as written, I armed myself, opened the cage and blocked
the light. My heart was going so fast I thought if the beast did
not kill me I would keel over from the strain.

Like a lit girandole the creature tore out of the cage, bouncing
violently about with a blistering roar. I think I can say, with a
little pride, that I stood my ground and kept the thing in focus,
although I doubt I could have heard myself scream, so who
knows.

Then it was gone. Thank the Lord for the anticlimax.

It spun right out of the front doors, directly into the bright
sunlight and kept right on going. Its bellow continued ricocheting
between the rocks until the noise ground down to a faint rumble.
Why didn't the sunlight freeze it? Must be something special
about the light beam in the Church. I no longer know what the
rules are anymore. When I think I am getting a handle on them,
they change abruptly.

I remained quiet for longer than was necessary, listening until
my ears throbbed for the return of the beast. The sound of the
wind; nothing more.

It took me two tries to let go of the shotgun.

I went into the cage, fighting back the irrational fear that
something else would come along and lock me inside the damn
thing. I opened the box. No puzzle answer, but a number of
heavy glass prisms. It took me about half an hour to figure
out how the pieces fitted together to form a single, somewhat
flower-shaped form. I set the glass on top of the staff, where
it fit nicely, setting onto the wood about 3/4 of an inch. Since

the staff was already in its hole in front of the pulpit, the light beam struck the glass squarely, sending a pure shaft over to the Bible quote on the wall. The word "faith" was illuminated. Thus endeth the goddamn lesson.

The astute reader—and I imagine whoever will find this and make it this far must be fairly astute (or credulous)—will notice that the word so boldly presented has less than eight letters. Being fairly astute myself, I picked up the staff and rotated it until it could fit back down into the hole which, since it is slightly ovoid, meant turning it 180 degrees. The light beam shot off onto the opposite wall, deftly illuminating a blank patch of wood. Wonderful.

I might be here a while, yet.

Until I figure out what's what, I am shutting the front doors.

Sep. 24th, 2004 02:39 pm Entry 43

It's beautiful. I suppose I should

I feel like a randy teen again and words in ink just seem too grown up.

I found a way off of the mountain quicker than I thought I would. And as you can tell from the grass stain on this page, I am in a completely new land. At first, I thought I materialized in one of the lush valleys that I could see from near the Church, but the sun, the COLORS

The beam of light either shone on the word "faith", or a bare patch of wall. After touching the spot for raised markings or faint scratchings, it occurred to me to try and extrapolate the beam as if the wall were not there. I (cautiously) ventured outside, listening for the Whirligig From Hell all the while, and eyeballed an educated guess as to where the beam would land. I walked to the spot, rolled one rock from another and there it was, carved out of the rock as if someone, somehow, had drawn their finger through soft mud.

DISGUISE

There is a monster of a storm rolling over the horizon (actual weather!) so I should wrap this up before it gets too dim, or wet. So far, I have not found a light source in the Temple, although the mirror there does shimmer very very faintly. God, I have a good feeling about this place. It is so full of vitality, such a difference from the other places, even the Swamp... but it is not just vitality, it is

I hate to say it, as if ashamed of my civilized tastes, but things look manicured (but not quite)... orderly (almost)... like I popped into an enormous, yet natural park built on the scale of giants. Yet, the appeal is also that the place is so wild, so vivid, energetic.

I knew a woman named Rubina—really—back in, (damn, I miss my other diaries) maybe 1979. When I was first introduced to her it was at a fancy dress function, which, it turned out, was not Rubina's normal environment. She was amazing, honestly breathtaking in her magnificent gown, but what really captivated me was her lusty, earthy, barroom nature barely contained beneath the restraints of the social atmosphere. I later learned (because she told me in considerable detail, weeks later) that she was an ex-prostitute (she said "whore") who now gave it away for free with anyone who met her standards—which were fairly high but hardly unreachable, since I managed it, bless her heart—and who now earned her wages in the U.S. Forestry Service. She was in her early 40's at the time. I credit her with jump-starting my taste for older women. She was as different from the females I had surrounded myself with at the time as an authentic beer stein is from a china tea cup.

This place reminds me of Rubina.

Sep. 28th, 2004 03:34 pm Entry 44

I was without this journal for a few days, as I did not want to risk it while wading through a wide stream—a wise choice, it turned out, as I unexpectedly went in over my head twice. The crackers did not survive.

I have five blisters to show for it, including one the size of a baby's hand, but I am back from an eventful exploration of this spectacular wilderness. I have paid a price, though, as my former shirt is now officially a rag, my shoes are rotting and I am having some trouble walking. My feet are a mess, but I have had worse. They will be better in a few more days.

I reread what I just wrote. This place just seems to impart a sense of adventurous optimism, to coin a phrase. Here I am: walking is excruciating, my dreams have been weird distillations of color and sexual imagery (which is very unusual for me), I have encountered animals here that clearly could have killed me if they so chose, and I am in real danger of losing my shoes to mildew and wear. The beauty of this land seems to overpower most other emotions. I get the feeling that I should be more concerned than I am.

The storm on the horizon I had written about in the previous entry was slow to arrive, but amazing in its dark violence. It reminded me uncomfortably of the creature in the Church, without the agility. There was little rain, but fantastic bolts of sheer force struck seemingly within a hundred yards of the Temple, where I had chosen to cower. No, that's not fair. The storm could easily have fried me until very crisp. I am still guilty about my reaction to the black creature.

The statue here might help explain the sexual dreams. Made from a gorgeous green marble (the same material as the Temple), there are two figures instead of one. A man and a woman, they are naked and locked in an exceedingly carnal embrace. He is standing holding her, while she has wrapped her legs tightly around his hips. It is dynamic, visceral and definitely not something one would find in a public park. It is also profoundly disturbing, although that fact did not register until I had returned from my hike. I have found myself staring at it; becoming more and more creeped out, as my daughter would say, the longer I study it.

I am looking at it now.

Her face is the first sign that something is amiss. Slightly Asian in cast, her expression is intense. I have seen reflections of that countenance in women a half-second away from climax, so that is what I assumed the artist had intended. But studying it closely, I see that more is going on, much more. She is in deep mental anguish. Not merely frightened, she is experiencing horror, or terrible despair. I imagine she is within a moment of orgasm, after having learned an hour before of her husband's death sentence (cancer?)—or, having poisoned her beloved without his knowledge? The last sex before a suicide pact?

Christ, so much for "adventurous optimism." The longer I am near the statue, though, the more it raises my hackles.

Part of it is that HIS face is entirely covered by her long hair. Entirely. No features whatsoever. His identity is a complete blank of marble strands. He's tallish, with a lean, muscular swimmer's body. His rear is clenched in sexual tension. His arms are holding her as closely as possible, his legs are in a wide stance.

It's hard to believe that any sculptor would deliberately create such a life-sized study in

Oh, Lord, I think I see the connection. I need to test something.

Sep. 30th, 2004 06:39 pm Entry 45

The Temple is a solid, cylindrical structure apparently built from extremely well-fitted blocks of green marble. The entryway (par for the course, there is only one) is an open rectangle half again my height—and contains the only right angles I can see in the place. The roof is a dome, again somehow made from fitted pieces of highly polished stone. There are seven pillars around the Temple, though I do not know enough architecture to tell if they are necessary or decorative.

Inside is dark and full of echoes, yet vaguely luminescent, like an ice cave. What light streams inside reveals a round, smooth and largely barren interior. The floor looks barely trod upon.

The only furniture is a sizable, full-body oval mirror in a baroque wooden frame, including hinged stand, plus a graceful gray pedestal cupping an intriguing black sphere about ten inches across. Touching the sphere produces a startling result, which I will get to below. On the back of the mirror's frame is written a verse. Both items look entirely out of place here.

The verse, in English, appears to be black or maroon ink on wood:
Love may fill this cup
as blood inspires the anima
whether driving spears
or, shaking, the caress,
inventing hasty alibi...
The One and his echo.
The first... the Last... emotion.

Writing about the statue made a connection. While I still feel the statue has much more subtext than I am understanding (Hell, likely all the statues mean more than I can apprehend right now), it also seems to be a clue to the verse. I was about to put the combination PASSION into the key, when I quickly realized that has one too few letters. I tried PASSIONS, instead, and got no reaction.

Once again, though, talking to myself like a lunatic has benefits, here. Speaking the word "passion" got results.

First, though, long before today, I touched the black ball in front of the mirror. Instantly, my pitiful reflection was replaced by a vivid moving image: a woman and, moving in and out of frame, an elderly man inside what looked like a private study or old-fashioned office. She was thoughtfully searching through a large book, occasionally speaking with the gentleman. There was no sound. While the periphery of the image dissolved into fuzzy gray blotches, most of the image was quite clear.

And although she's older and had her hair pinned up, I am 90% certain she is the woman in the painting. The "The Crime" painting. Seeing her gives me an ache just behind my breastbone.

Why can I not recognize her? It is driving me insane. ("Short trip," my daughter's voice says in my mind)

It gave me a massive headache after a minute, so I let my hand slip from the sphere. Today, though, my intoning the word "passion" made the surface of the mirror go murky, like flowing mud at dusk. After about five minutes it cleared back to a simple reflection. Not a very helpful reaction, but an interesting one. I went out to check the statue, but there was no change.

I am going to go restock my food supplies, then experiment some more with the mirror. I need to get to the bottom of this.

Who is that woman?!

Oct. 1st, 2004 08:46 pm Entry 46

It is a bizarre, so-tragic-it's-comical feeling: my feet are raw and bleeding—they so remind me of uncooked steak that I am actually having hunger pangs and fantasies involving gas grills.

I have heard people say "I'd kill for a hamburger." No they would not. I would, though.

I have not been back to the Temple since my last entry. I tried soaking my abused feet in the tubs at the Mansion, but that hurt far more than I expected it to. I am crawling as often as walking; my shoes have been abandoned.

Those were not children in the car, in the "dream". Anya, Erica and Nathan must be the names of the people who were in the car with me. They were (are) adults. They were compatriots, or friends, or something. I would bet a new pair of shoes that the woman in the mirror was either Anya or Erica.

I need to get back to the Temple. See what else can be seen.

It amazes me how blithely I now accept the existence of what seem to be magic mirrors and words of power. Adapt or die, I guess.

When I was ten or so I learned how to walk on my hands. It might be time to revisit that skill, wrote the 53 year old man.

Damn.

Oct. 3rd, 2004 03:29 am Entry 47

In my 40's, before my book repair hobby abruptly became a career change, I had worked at a law firm. I used to be employed as a senior researcher in a mid-sized practice in the District of Columbia. I had an office with a pleasant view, albeit through a fairly small window. The management had been slow in embracing computers; while there had been plans to install a terminal for years, sitting on my desk was an electric typewriter of the kind just short of a word processor. My desk had been just about as wooden, polished and old-fashioned as the firm itself. Nearly encircling the small room had been an entire brigade of thick books; references — some a little esoteric for a firm that principally handled environmental and corporate cases — most of which had been read (and in two cases written) from cover to cover. The floor had cheap carpet, the ceiling expensive light fixtures, and the walls a tan and cobalt blue striped wallpaper.

I am in that office now.

...except that where the window used to be is now wallpaper with a rectangular dark spot, as if a painting had been removed recently. And where the door used to be is now a full-length mirror. The books are gone. My daughter's picture is still in a frame on the desk, but there is no typewriter. My silver-plated pen set is in a drawer along with fine writing paper, but none of the paperwork I associated with that job—which I had left before I had turned 50—is in existence. There are some unusual postage stamps, though. Also, some square manilla envelopes, a maroon ink bottle, a few candies with exotic wrappers I think may be from Mexico, a blank postcard showing a beach scene with "Baja California Sunset" in big green letters and a not-so-blank postcard.

I have sat here, dumbly I am sure, for the last who knows how long. Earlier today (yesterday?) I said "passion" to the mirror in the Temple. Once again it became murky, as if the light falling upon it grew sluggish and dirty. Before it reverted back I touched the black sphere. The image cleared, showing this facsimile of my office. I stared intently for a while, memories fighting with both hands to try to reach the surface; nothing happened, but so real was the illusion that I felt compelled to reach for the glass.

Here I am—trapped in a recursive nightmare, every step toward an answer actually a step deeper into confusion, into conflicting memories, into blind impossibility.

I only now

The second postcard r

Addressed to my home, the second postcard reads:

"*Avery,*
I am so sorry to hear about Robin. I cannot imagine your pain, love. We have all lost people in this, but to survive a child... Nathan told me about your suspicions. Please know that I am always available through the usual channels. I am fifteen pages into the book you leant to me. My great uncle sends his deepest sympathies.
Always Yours,
Erica"

The postcard reads so familiar but I know I know I know I know please my daughter is alive

Oct. 5th, 2004 04:31 am Entry 48

I had no problem leaving the mock-office. I stepped back through the mirror. Indeed, I have returned, as it is late and the light is very good here.

I have run out of options as far as the keyword for the next area. Certainly, the damned postcard is written as if it were in code, but I have had no luck so far in figuring it. I mean, in the middle of condolences, a mention of being fifteen pages into a book?

I am at a loss, though. I have searched as much as my blistered feet will carry me.

Now that there are reflective surfaces about, I have noticed that I look absolutely terrible. No shirt, no shoes, pants with holes, a blanket or two always in a state of almost slipping off my shoulders. I look thirty pounds thinner, at least (want to lose weight? Eat the same things for weeks). I have a spot smack in the center of my forehead I had never noticed before, like the red dot some Indian woman wear. All right, not quite like that, but it is a reddish scabbed over little dent.

On top of everything, my food stores are getting noticeably low. Oh, I still have a couple of weeks eating three meals a day, but those last couple of meals will be nothing but soda crackers.

I have tried using the black sphere (without having said "passion" first) to spy on the woman I saw earlier, but while I get a sense of it attempting to show me something, the image is mottled and distorted. I wonder if she figured out she was being viewed, or if there are places where I cannot see her. Or the sphere is... what, out of magic? Power? Tokens?

Had a nap, just now. Didn't help. Tired. Can barely read my handwriting. Feeling old.

Oct. 6th, 2004 01:53 am Entry 49

I have burned daylight by alternately tearing my hair out trying to come up with the next goddamn keyword, then just collapsing on the ground outside of the Temple, soaking up sunlight in the hopes, I suppose, that it will replace the despair that threatens. Regrettably, it turns out that HERE I can get sunburned. Fortunately I caught this before it got too bad. Small favors. I have nearly used up the antiseptic from the Swamp's medical kit just on my battered feet. It looks to be worth the trouble, though. Now I just need to stay off of them for a while, which is hard to do. I get very restless when I am not wallowing in mad depression.

I am amazed I am writing in this book now, honestly. I can not find my center anymore. The postcard has shaken me to my core. I swing wildly between being convinced the whole thing is a sham of code, or else believing deeply that its news is real and that somehow all my recent memories of my daughter are false or out-of-date.

Really though, come on—I would remember her death, yes? How the Hell could I not?

Still... I can only wonder as I reread this journal for the tenth time. I notice little things, like how I rarely mention Robin by name (almost always calling her "my daughter"), as if by writing "Robin" I run the risk of not recognizing to whom I refer. How I have never Jesus Christ

I have never mentioned my grandchildren by name, their real names their real names are

I have just done a very bad thing

Oct. 6th, 2004 04:04 pm Entry 50

I'm afraid I lost it. Had a fit. My life as I remember it is unraveling hour by hour.

don't remember

I tore up the office pretty badly. Overturned the desk, ripped the wallpaper, smashed things.

I destroyed the postcard. Yes, the written one, the one that likely had the only clue to get me out of here. I almost smashed the mirror, but realizing what that might have meant snapped me out of it.

I might be able to no, no the postcard is a lost cause. I did a heck of a number on it.

You'll notice this page is in different ink. That is because I ruined my pen, too. I am writing with the silver-plated one, now, that used to be on the desk.

Sitting here, in the entrance of the Temple, watching another storm roll slowly in this direction, sucking on one of the candies I found in the office, peacefully numb. But not so in shock that I have missed what I have done. I have sunk my own boat.

Storm is getting closer.

Oct. 7th, 2004 03:54 pm Entry 51

Dream. I think it was a dream

In an apartment—small, cozy, lots of green. Seemed somewhat familiar. I was with two people, friends or coworkers, we were just getting ready to leave for somewhere. For some reason I lift an overturned coffee mug on the kitchen counter, only to be surprised by an eyeball—glistening, pulsing—underneath it. I am dismayed, startled, but calm. I stare at it, it stares at me.

I turn to let the others know, but this time get a bad scare when instead of the coworkers I see the image of my imperfect twin (described before), all bound and blind, hanging from nothing so only his toes are touching the carpet.

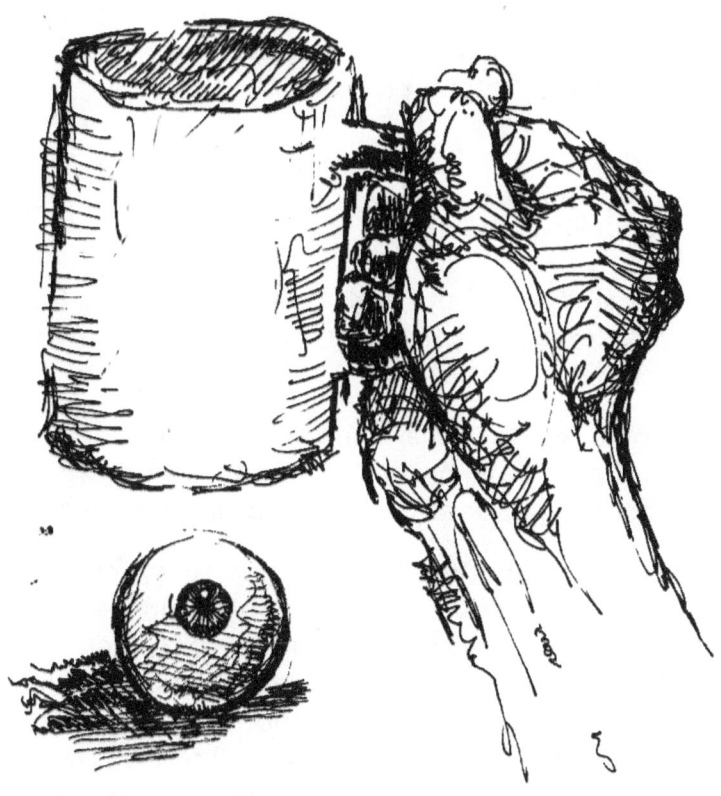

He's facing me, only three feet away. Extremely real, in torturous pain, twitching as if ants were crawling in and out of him.

Struggling.

Oct. 9th, 2004 11:58 pm Entry 52

The last day or so has been spent in a haze. I can only imagine what I looked like or exactly what I did. I even came to lucidity while knee-deep in the Seltzer Sea, just outside the Cave, without any memory of how I got there or what I thought I had been doing. Later, I gave myself a cold fright when I could not find the key. I discovered it after a panicked search lying among the dried fruit, probably tossed there absently as I was plodding about like a zombie.

Or a dementia patient.

I also found that I had, at some point during my daze, written on the "Baja California" blank postcard:

"Erica,

This is Avery. I am not well. I am not sure who you are, or what has happened to me. Please, help me."

I had even dated it and put simply "Erica" in the address field. As a return address I wrote (in tiny script for some reason), "The Temple by the two statues"

I will be sure to get that out as soon as I find the nearest drop box. In the meantime I have been considering my options; I suspect this is responsible for many of my deep, downward spirals.

It is hopeless, is it not? I have no way to go forward. By the time my feet are up to another long bout of aimless exploration, I will have run out of food. The idea of sitting back and waiting for a withering death is as unappealing as it sounds, but I don't know how to proceed! This is not how I expected to finish this—I was strong and lucky enough to find food, tend to fairly nasty wounds, hold on to something resembling sanity while everything I thought I knew changed unrecognizably and

My mind is spinning in tight, ivory circles. how poetic, wonder where that came from

I guess there is nothing more to do except put the card in the post, wherever that might be, and hope the U.S. Mail does pickup here in Sheer Delirium. I wonder if I spared one or two of those weird stamps during my rampage.

Oct. 13th, 2004 12:05 am Entry 53

The stamps may be odd, but they do not do anything special.

I have had very little to write about, until now. I broke my poor brain on the "passion" verse, trying out every combination I could think of. Did you know if you take the last letter of the first word of every line, plus the last letter of the last word, you get an anagram of "renegers?" You do. I did. Does not work on the key. In such ways do I drive myself insane.

I have had no more success at spying on the woman in the mirror. I wonder if that is just as well.

So. I was in the office, spinning my mental wheels in the tacky grease of despair when I discovered myself lying upon the dusty floor. I was staring up at the ceiling, underneath the shelving, etc., letting my eyes wander in step with my mind, when I noticed that the shelving, the now broken desk (which I have since set upright) and even the wallpaper all had tiny little company marks tucked away on them. "Quartile Manufacturing." Now, so very few things are commercial in these places (and then mostly the food) that I took notice—especially when I saw that "Quartile" had eight letters. I bolted out, tried in on the key and... nothing. Crap.

I thought about it some more. I began to understand how much revenge may motivate the creators of this place.

I am ecstatic to report that I have escaped the Temple.

Oct. 15th, 2004 12:01 am Entry 54

I am on a roll, although I am beginning to truly worry about just how many of these "places" there could be.

After having dialed REQUITAL into the key I popped into an exceedingly bright, sunny place, which blinded me for a minute. I was on a dry, scrubby savanna, blisteringly hot. My healing feet started to burn almost instantly, so I hopped rapidly to the nearest shade. It was so seriously quiet at first that it crossed my mind that I had gone partially deaf. After a moment, however, I could hear a few quiet insects and, way off in the distance, the call of what I thought was a bird. On the horizon in one direction were a hazy range of low? mountains, shimmering in the heat. A few thready clouds barely graced a very earthish sky. A light breeze made the temperature just bearable, but only when I had found shade; remember, I was naked except for pants, a blanket and a tattered makeshift bag for my few supplies.

The shade was provided by what must have been the "statue" for the area: a boxy, wooden carriage with large wood-and-steel wheels. All it needed was a horse and a driver, but both were conspicuously lacking. Unlike the carriages I have seen or read about, this one only had an entrance in the back—a little door. Above the door was painted "HOME".

I wish.

Inside was stifling, but at least I got completely out of the sun. By that time I was sweating profusely. Instead of seats there were rows of small, lipped shelves, all containing rows of tiny glass bottles. Each bottle was labeled, indicating the contents. Such contents included wormwood, turmeric, spearmint, verbena, birch bark, etc.etc. There were 102 in all!

On the bottom of each bottle was a seemingly random pair of letters, e.g. SO, HS, AM, and so on. It did not take my now experienced, if baking, brain too long to understand the next word was somehow to be found under those bottles.

It took me the rest of the day and all of the night (by imported candle light) to figure it out, but by that time I had become convinced that visiting this place should only be done during the merely simmering darkness. HOME—the first label that started with "H" had the letters SP, the first with "O" had the letters IR, and so on, until I got SPIRITUS. I did not think that a word, at first, but it worked in the key.

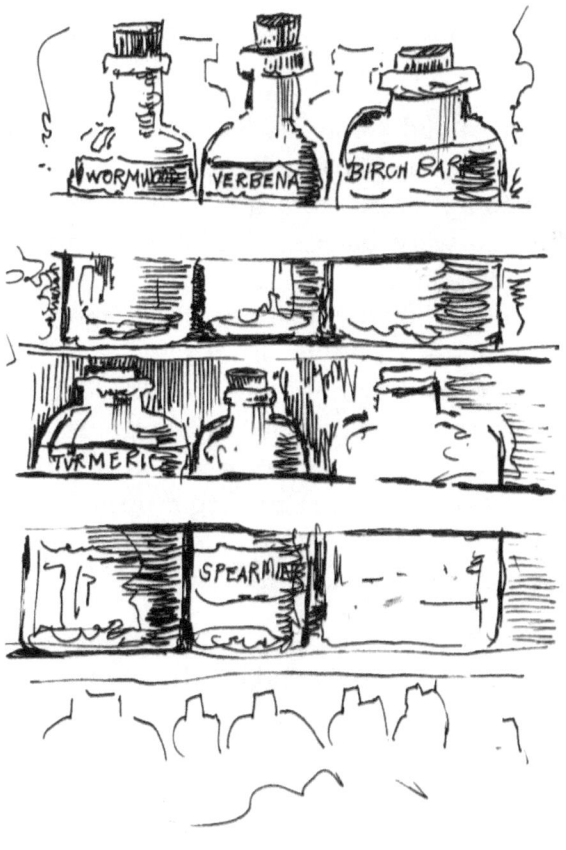

And now I am writing this in the same, desolate installation that contained the Guard Post. Wonderful.

But at least it is air-conditioned.

I have been avoiding the newfound place like the plague. I was too flip, last entry. The area is terrifying. It is, without a doubt in my mind, in the same installation as the Guard Post, but instead of being safely enclosed from the horrors on the monitors, as near as I could tell I was WITH the horrors. Long, very wide corridors looked designed for vehicular traffic. At least one—for I have done very little exploration—rose upwards ten or twelve degrees. I got the strong impression of being entirely underground. The primary noise was the asthmatic blowing of the ventilation system, although there were the occasional electronic beeps, the insectile flicker of a dying florescent light, as well as less identifiable sounds that seemed like they were right around the next corner.

The statue was close by, so THAT I can describe: simultaneously out-of-place, yet obviously carved to order, it was made from the same lacquered wood as the ones in the Swamp and the Guard Post.

She stood upon a wooden pedestal, feet well apart. Her hands reached the low ceiling. It is a good thing they did, too, for it was apparent from her expression that she's holding it up. Her arms were bare and thick with muscles, for a female. Indeed, she looked for all the world like one of those bodybuilders you see during the off-hours of a sports network. She appeared to be a tall example of Irish or Scottish stock, judging from her features. Her hair was shoulder-length and tousled to the point of rattiness. She wore bell-bottoms, sandals and a what I think is called a sports bra nowadays. She had the breasts of a fourteen year old, despite seeming around thirty or forty. Probably thirty. Her face is screwed up in intense concentration, strain and perhaps pain. A female Atlas.

The most interesting detail, to me, was the (carved) tattoo of a male lion's head on the small of her back. It was not in mid-roar, but looked peaceful instead.

It sounds silly, but her presence was so reassuring in an incredibly creepy place that I could not do anything but hover around her. If I could have hired her as a bodyguard I would have sold my library for the funds.

As it is, I am writing this by the very different statue of the pregnant warrior, next to the Cave. The sun is out and fails to burn, the Sea hisses pleasantly...

The lack of food will motivate me to explore sooner rather than later, of course. I am taking the shotgun and all the ammo I can carry, though.

Oct. 18th, 2004 12:18 am Entry 56

I have found the bodies. The ones I saw on the monitors.

I am writing this in a mess hall of the Installation, which is my name for this Hellhole. The mess is very well lit, has only one working door that I can watch all the time, as well as a considerable supply of mostly useless foodstores. Fortunately, about ten percent of it is nonperishable or otherwise unspoiled, so I have been able to add some variety to my diet: wheat bread; canned corn, peas, beets; stale corn flakes; and a sack of dried beans that I am determined to cook, even though it has probably been thirty years since I have boiled dried beans. I remember that you have to soak them for a while...

Wandering with extreme caution, I have yet to completely discover the limits to this place. My sore feet are not quite up to briskly exploring what must be at least a mile of corridors and side rooms. Nor, to be honest, is my courage.

Setting the scene—at the end of one hallway are three security doors, each with an expertly ominous red warning light blinking soundlessly away. Each door has a narrow, strongly reinforced window. One is covered, but the other two reveal a darkened lab or conference room, scattered with decomposed human bodies. Both rooms also have something else inside that is very much alive and active, despite not having anything I could see that resembled heads. I clutched my shotgun and backed away.

It is the tension of meeting one of those things that keeps my attention snapping back over my shoulder.

On the bright side, there have not been any human remains on this side of the security doors, anywhere. I found this mess hall, thank God, as well as two racquetball courts (honestly), a television room with a plasma screen that only picks up a strange sort of static, what seemed like a surprisingly low-tech chemical lab, a machine shop

Man. It is about a half-hour after I wrote "shop" above. There had been an unholy squeal some distance away that could have been metal being torn apart. Showing more courage than I felt,

I went to see what it could have been, shotgun at the ready. I could not find a thing, although I did not scour the area room by room. I think I will grab some items from the mess and retreat to the Mansion, where I might try my hand at cooking some beans.

fifteen minutes later can't find the statue

shit how could I be lost?

Oct. 19th, 2004 05:11 pm Entry 57

I am safely in the Mansion. The fact that this place has no doors leading out used to be claustrophobic, but right now it is enormously comforting.

The sloping corridors of the Installation are deceptive. I had wandered onto another level without intending to, so when I tried to find my way back I was actually one story higher than I knew. It gave the word "dread" a fresh new meaning.

Anyway.

I have some beans bubbling away on the excellent wood stove here. I do not have a lot to spice them with, but it will be a marvel just to have hot food again. When I got out of the service I thought I would never truly miss beans again, but much time has passed and my circumstances are... different...

I feel like my head is physically floating several inches about my neck. My sight seems somehow disconnected from my

I don't know. What it meant to be "me" has fundamentally changed since the Temple and I am uncertain if I can adapt, or even understand.

Finally, the beans are done. Ran out of water a little early, but burning just gives them flavor, right?

Eat first, then digest.

Who am I, if I do not have my memories?

I think about the time I was watching my daughter in a municipal swimming pool. She was four. Her small hands had been clinging to the cement lip while she energetically bobbed up and down, having a ball. Then she slipped, went under, came back up, went under a second time...

I rapidly went to the edge, dropped to my belly, thrust both arms into the blue water and lifted her into the air. She had had the same expression I was probably wearing: almost equal parts panic and bemusement. We both got a little scare, just a small one, but while I had been confident of my ability to rescue her, she at just that moment had her first young taste of mortal danger—her first brush with death, it could be argued.

We both had recovered quickly and the day went on (although she was finished with the pool for the time being). And of course she continued to be a little girl for some years afterward.

But she was never quite the same since that late morning in the water. Oh, I am sure few people ever noticed, but a parent does; her demeanor had been displaced just a fraction. I could see it in her eyes. I still can, when I close mine.

Or can I?

How real can memory be when it melts so easily? How solid is a person when, as the sum of their memories, they find out just how much is base fiction?

When I get an urge to record in this journal the only time a woman struck me, or when I found a gold coin glued into the binding of a Steinbeck first edition, or the last words Marian spoke to me before the hospital elevator closed in our faces...

If my daughter is dead, how could I not know? If she's gone, who

Who am I?

Oct. 26th, 2004 06:01 pm Entry 59

I am consolidating some of the more cryptic facts and passwords so far:

1. The House, Seltzer Sea, white stone, small woman stepping into air, (unknown)

2. The Mansion, Seltzer Sea (probably), no statue, PYMANDER

3. The Shack, Swamp, lacquered wood, zaftig African, DOCTRINE

4. The Cave, Seltzer Sea, white stone, pregnant warrior, ALCHEMIC

5. The Guard Post, Swamp (probably), lacquered wood, Conan-like brooder w/ necklace, HERMETIC

6. The Church, Aerie, tawny stone, priest with staff, MYSTICAL

7. The Temple, Pastoral, green marble, intense embracing couple, DISGUISE

8. The Wagon, ???, pine? and steel wagon with 102 herbal bottles, REQUITAL

9. The Installation, Swamp (probably), lacquered wood, powerlifter woman, SPIRITUS

I have made (and eaten) several batches of beans, now. I stirred my last can of meat into the latest pot, creating something that, if I had been served that in the Army I would have puked, but here I devoured it with a quavering relish. My stomach has not protested at the new influx of stick-to-my-ribs food as much as I anticipated; must be toned by all the weeks of dried fruit.

Braced as I am with hot meals, I am going back to the Installation tonight or tomorrow.

I found some clothes!

Some sort of small supply room opened with difficulty (earlier I had thought it completely stuck) to reveal a veritable trove of... well, mostly stuff useless to me, but some interesting finds, including several uniforms hanging in a closet. It is a little odd to wear dress slacks with no underwear, but not one complaint will I voice on the subject.

Best of all, there are shoes and socks. The left shoe of one pair fit very well, while the right of an other did the same. Dry socks, sturdy shoes. The only thing better now would be hiking boots.

The pocket of my uniform says "Abborazh". All the shirts have that stitched into the breast pocket. No, does not work on the key, nor does it seem to be an anagram. A number of things are labeled in here, all in English, sort of. The words are usually English, but the word order is strange.

An example: a heavy, locked metal container very like an ammunition box reads GREASE TO KILL, then VERY COMFORT IN WATER. It is like a bad translation.

Some words just seem to be nonsense, like Abborazh. On a plain, military-issue carton containing evil-smelling soap (I think) is the simple phrase "Amszuo Spill". Okay, then. For all I know, "Abborazh" means "shirt". Though I doubt it. Whe

Christ. There is a high screech that happens just infrequently enough that I become complacent, until it scares the shit out of me again. It sounds like a poorly maintained machine doing some major lifting, except—this is the unnerving part—it does not always come from the same direction. The one time I went investigating I came to a dead end. In fact, it

footsteps

Nothing. This place is NOT good for my nerves, but I will be damned before I run away from phantoms.

Well, it has been about an hour since I would swear I heard

footsteps echoing down the hallway outside this supply room. Except for the ever-present hum of the air system, it has been quiet. It is possible that the sameness of the corridors and the white noise in every direction is causing a sensory deprivation, leading to auditory hallucinations.

Hell. I did not believe it even as I wrote it.

I have mixed feelings about footsteps. Anywhere but here, they would probably be welcome. But after what I have witnessed, anything still alive here would not

Damn it to Hell. That's it. Walking dead or not, it is going to get its leg broken.

Oct. 29th, 2004 11:57 pm Entry 61

It is noticeably easier to act the brave explorer when you have a military shotgun in your hands. Man, though, do those things get heavy after a while. Another thing the movies gloss over.

Frustrated and angry, I took off after the phantom sounds before the ink dried on my previous entry.

Phantom, indeed; I quickly lost track of their direction, which goes some distance to suggest they really are hallucinations. I had worked up a head of steam, however, and damned if not having any quarry was going to keep me from a proper hunt.

It was in this frame of mind when I barged into a library.

I can understand why I had not found it previously: it was at the end of a corridor displaying more than its share of blinking warning signs. It just occurred to me now that those might have been deliberate.

The library was clearly not part of the Installation, as such. The books were in plain English, Russian and more than a couple in Hebrew. The room contained decorations, embellishments and obviously "alien" gadgets (more on those in a minute). The books are going to keep me occupied for a while, I can tell—just skimming through them has broadened my horizons.

For instance, one was written by me. I have only the vaguest memory of writing a critique of the popularization of astrology in modern Western culture. My recollection would have it that it was something I had recommended to me, not a text I had obviously researched and had published. The book assumes, to put it too simply here, that astrology is a real and noble Art, badly misrepresented by charlatans and ignorant bumpkins in the popular media, including (especially!) those that support it.

Do tell. I had no idea.

There were these weird little retro-tech boxes with brass rivets and tiny windows. Peering inside a couple, I saw what looked like little animal brains floating in preservative. Truly odd. Each brain had a delicate weave of silver threads around it.

Saving the most interesting for last, there were also four figurines, each about nine inches high, carved from I have no idea, perhaps a very hard wood, and painted expertly.

All male, the first one was a handsome, wild-haired, slightly swarthy man in white armor and a white cape, brandishing a serious sword and looking pissed.

Figurine two was a decidedly genial gentleman, red hair in loose curls both on his head and as a beard. Heavyish, he was dressed well in the manner of a European sophisticate, except with little touches (like a plaid tie) that brought him a tad more down-to-earth. He carried a French horn in one hand as if he were just off to the park to play a bit by the lake.

Figurine three was a black, hip young man who still had an aura of age or wisdom about him. His afro was done in a close box cut. A gold earring was in his left ear. He wore mostly dark reds and grays with bright yellow accents. Everything was sharp enough to pass into a posh New York nightclub, but more as the owner/manager than a mere patron. His hands were as wide open as his arms. He appeared delighted to see you.

The last one was just about the opposite, in some ways, as #3: thin, very pale, everything in black and silver, slightly androgynous—what the kids call Goth nowadays, I suppose. Very long black hair fell straight down to his hips. There was a skull motif, particularly on his chest; although I must say his eyes did not look unfriendly, neither would I want to meet him in a dark alley. Or here, even. His left hand held a silver cup horizontally.

I am going back to this room soon, but right now I am writing this in the comfort and safety of the Cave. I needed a change of air.

I hope this is only the beginning of the revelations.

Nov. 3rd, 2004 11:56 pm Entry 62

I have been camping out in the library, steadfastly reading what I could and ignoring the occasional scrape of clawed foot just outside the wonderfully secure door.

My principle hurdles have been sensory deprivation (how did people WORK here?), the need for bathroom breaks (the nearest one being over three minutes away, which does not sound like much until you try it in a desolate underground nightmare) and, most disturbingly, blinding headaches.

The headaches have been illuminating in their own right, however. They recur only with certain books, or even particular pages in certain books. Latin will sometimes, but not always, set it off. When it does, that particular passage/page/book will always do it—pow, my forehead throbs as if I had poured hot tar into my sinuses. It lasts for around 15 minutes, more or less.

Back to the books: this library is to a typical New Age bookstore what the Protected Archive section of, say, Oxford U. is to a

Waldenbooks. I had never imagined the enormous amount of dry, academic detail that could go into a 500-page description of the "33 Facets of Upper Node Numistrophy" or "Geomancy as a Path to Para-Iconic Realization".

For the most part it is fantastically pedantic gibberish, although it does suggest the hidden existence of university-level formal instruction in such esoteric topics, somewhere. It is just that I have never seen diplomas boasting a Ph.D. in Numerology hanging in a professional's office.

The four statuettes I wrote about are also more than they seem; on particular surfaces they create a kind of glow, a luminescence. I have only just started playing around with this. More later.

Just as well, though. I think I am done with the books.

Nov. 5th, 2004 09:36 pm Entry 63

I had a vivid, elaborate dream earlier this morning.

I was searching about in a murkier version of the Installation. Things were befogged by a miasma of fine, wet particles. The architecture had grotesque, baroque touches. One that sticks in my memory was a large, wall-mounted statue of a grinning devil holding a cornucopia-like horn, which was empty save for a bright light.

I entered an octagonal room to discover two figures on the far side. Both were cloaked in shadow, but the left hand one gestured for me to come forth. Between them were six steps leading up to a wall with writing on it.

I slowly approached the beckoning figure. The darkness parted enough for me to see that it was the Goth figurine, except full-sized and in the flesh. He stood half-a-head taller than me, which I remember surprised me. His expression was unreadable. I was about to say something when he beat me to it.

"The measure of a man is how he faces his fears," he said in a rather dry voice.

I looked up the stairs. I still could not read the writing.

"Is that the word for the next world?" I asked.

He nodded, although in such a way as to suggest I had asked the wrong question. I heard the clink of metal. The figure to the right revealed itself, becoming my "bound twin". I noticed with a start that his blindfold was slipping; I could almost see one of his eyes.

I turned back to the Goth. He waited patiently. I started upon the stairs.

There were only six of them, but setting my foot on the first one was difficult—the second was painful. It was an enormous effort to make my left foot touch the third step, by which time I noticed my body (and clothes) had begun to fade. More accurately, my being was decomposing into little dark, wet particles.

I turned to the Goth in a rising panic, but my vision had begun to fail, too. My heart raced. I called out, "Who are you?" to which he answered.

Then I woke up.

I am studying the statuettes before me. I believe I know who they are supposed to represent, in a postmodern sort of way: the Goth is Uriel, the man with the horn is Gabriel, the sword-wielder would be Michael... which leaves the snazzy black gentleman. Raphael?

Nov. 7th, 2004 12:53 am Entry 64

The library!

I have been away in the Cave after burning myself out with the books and the statuettes. I needed time in a peaceful setting thinking about that dream.

When I returned to the library, I stopped absolutely cold. Mentally, I began to subtract the solid, impressive bookcases—great wooden things that went from floor to ceiling and defined the general space. Most of them were against the walls, or so I thought. But after some mind's eye gymnastics and a bout or two of muscle strain, I discovered that some of the shelving actually stood before gaps created by the walls' odd angles.

It was the library. In my dream, the octagonal room. I had been studying for hours, DAYS inside an eight-sided room without realizing it.

After recovering from the shock of recognition, I stood by the entrance and imagined where that would place the two dark figures in my dream. At that spot stood an angled bookcase. Putting my meager weight into it (and happy for an outlet to the tension this damn place engenders), I completely failed to move the case. I jumped into the project of removing all the books (all 145 of them, on just that one case!), then, without even a moment's rest, tried moving the case again. I pushed it just enough to see that there was a flat, plain wall behind it. No steps, no word, no markings.

Only briefly discouraged, I spent 30 minutes forcing more and more books into the gap, very gradually increasing the space until my rail-like body could squeeze into and past it. I felt along the wall, hoping like an idiot that something would reveal itself spontaneously, rewarding me for my hard, clever work.

Nothing.

Well, almost. I could just imagine that the texture of the wall segment was ever so slightly different than the rest.

This went on for a while. Until...

Remember I mentioned a few nights ago how the statuettes created a glow on "certain surfaces"? By that I meant on the table where I found them, if I dragged their bases along the top, it left a dim, but definite trail of pale coldfire. The light faded rapidly, but was intriguing to play with. Each figure left the same sort of trail. It only worked on the table, plus each chair in the room.

They also worked on that one wall segment. And when I took Uriel in hand and ran it high, the word HUMANITY shone a ghostly yellow-white.

Sometimes it pays to follow your dreams.

Nov. 9th, 2004 10:47 pm Entry 65

I have been here a couple of days, now, and I still am not sure just where that is.

It is pleasant enough. I am waiting for the reveal of whatever disturbing feature this place has to offer, as all of these areas seem to possess at least one. There is a small adobe house, sitting attractively on a very broad desert valley. The sky is precisely Earth-like—I could be somewhere in New Mexico, for all I can tell.

The long axis of the adobe runs East-West. About fifty feet from the western end rests a patch of land that is slightly moist, suggesting a spring below, perhaps, that does not quite make it to the surface. There may have been a garden here, but if so it has been removed or baked out of existence. It would explain a couple of rusted iron poles at one end; might have supported a sun shade at one time. Otherwise, the plant life is mostly thorny bushes, small cacti and even smaller succulents. Fauna-wise, there are lots of little lizards, plus I found a snake skin. I will have to watch for them. There are plenty of ants, too. They tend to crawl up my legs.

I waited until daylight to arrive here, since the Swamp taught me about the possible hazards of popping into an unknown place at night. It is interesting: day and night seem to be in sync, no matter the universe I find myself inside.

The wind was blowing with vim when I materialized, but has since settled into a moderating breeze. The sky has been festooned with bright, fluffy clouds during the day, coldly brilliant (and very familiar) stars at night. If I am not on some corner of the world I was born to, it is a mighty acceptable simulacrum.

Predictably, though, it is as remote as Hell. No road leads up to the adobe. No airplanes fly overhead. It is pretty clear this place has not been visited for years.

The statue stands searching the hilly horizon, flattened left hand shading his brow while his right holds an old-fashioned lantern out about hip height. Everything except the steel lantern is made from weathered pine. I just realized those materials tie this area to the one with the wagon. He wears the gear of a seasoned traveler (good boots, for one thing) and his face is bearded and questioning. He must have lost his hat. It just seems he should have a hat.

Getting hungry. More on the adobe (and the oddly beautiful thing about the lantern) later.

Nov. 11th, 2004 03:29 am Entry 66

I am thinking I have discovered the region's one disturbing item. It will not seem so much, described with scratches of thin ink on paper, but, all the same...

I was standing in the doorway of the Adobe long after the sun had set. It would have been black as swamp water, had the lantern not been lit.

Yes, I had discovered during my first night that the statue's lamp burns with a fierce, white light after the night settles. It is a little too bright to look at directly. It throws into sharp relief everything within a 200 foot radius of the statue. The light is cold, perfectly silent, odorless. I thought, when I first witnessed it, that it was a little out of place; it did not fit within the setting of the dry, scurrying desert.

Last night, though, standing there, leaning slightly on the hard clay, the night seemed punctured. An eerie quality I simply could not put my finger on filled the desert air, saturating it. I grew more and more uneasy, as if I were staring directly at something that I simply could not (or would not) register. My mind began fashioning gross suggestions from the fringes of the illuminated sand. The very silence of the powerful light—no buzz of electricity, no oscillation of ballast, no crackle of fire—served to somehow blanket the rest of the night noises until nothing but ill-defined whispers remained.

I stood there, masochistically allowing the alien sense of reality to seep into my head. I had been feeling the formless panic that something was amiss slowly build just behind my sternum—

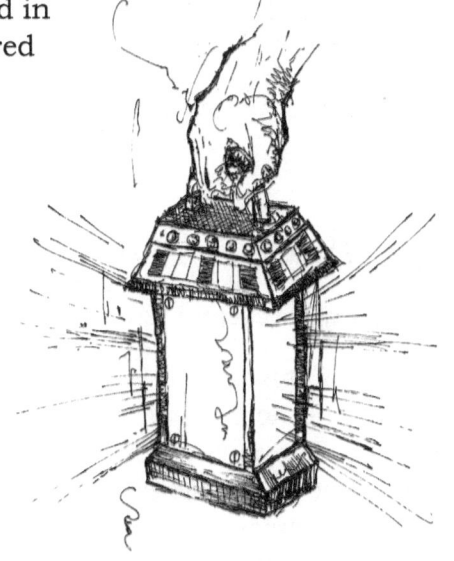

when the entire night crystalized in an instant. My focus was centered on the statue, unable to leave until my brain processed what had been right in front of it the entire damn time.

It is not going to seem like much. I debated about even committing this to paper.

The lamp was higher. Held higher. The carved statue was holding the lamp HIGHER.

Nov. 12th, 2004 11:59 pm Entry 67

Persistent, minor headache today.

Inside the Adobe it is comfortably furnished, or would be if someone had not taken the mattress off of the one single-sized bed. After shaking the dust and crud out of the two throw rugs, though, they made a serviceable covering for the strip frame.

Naturally, I did not have to sleep there. In fact, after my little revelation about the statue here, I slept in the Cave; my favorite space. Currently I am writing in the Mansion, since the light is so good. I still can not get used to not having a true shadow, though.

The Adobe has a little brush-burning stove, a small stock of drinking water (wishing for a pump or well, but there I am), five straw mats, a straw broom, a deck of Bicycle cards, what looks like an empty fishbowl, a flashlight with no bulb, several charcoal sticks, an easel, and four padded folding chairs. Two of the chairs sit on opposite sides of a simple wooden pedestal holding a game.

The game is a board divided by raised borders into 256 little white squares (16 X 16). One side has 16 square pieces, numbered 2-17. The other has round pieces painted with letters: A, C, D, E, G, I, K, L, N, O, P, R, S, T, U, Y. The board is otherwise unmarked.

As the Lord as my witness, I have no idea what any of it means.

Nov. 15th, 2004 02:52 am Entry 68

This is what happened.

I was dreaming vividly, again. Sitting at the game board in the Adobe, all the pieces in their current, real-life positions. Opposite me was Raphael, in the flesh. We began playing the game, as if I had known all along what the rules were. Things then took a decidedly more lucid turn. Here it is, as closely as I can recall it.

Raphael (moving a piece): "Number Four, four squares. Your turn."

Me (making my own move): "Letter Y, across from Number Six. Is this going to tell me the next word?"

R: "Yes. Number Thirteen, three squares then ten."

Me: "Ah, Letter I, to Number Two, then two over. Your Number Thirteen piece removed. Can I ask you a question? How is it that, when I first started this whole insane mess, I had to work until my ears bled to figure out each puzzle, but now I have angels handing the answers out to me in my dreams?"

R (laughs): "Number Fifteen to the nearest letter, which is your L. Removed. I am not an angel and no one is giving you the answers."

Me: "Letter G to Number Eight, then eight spaces. Then what has changed? How can I be divining the answers to hidden information? Why now, and not then?"

R: "I'm you, Avery. Uriel is you. You will meet Gabriel and, heaven help you, Michael, and they will all be you. Number Eight captures Letter G. You get a free move. You are just starting to remember the processes, that's all. Remember looking through that poker deck lying next to the bed, here?"

Me: "Uh, what? Yes. Why? Oh, um... Letter D over four spaces. And, uh, Letter I down two."

R: "That was you beginning to recall the process by which this game board gives the answer." (lifts both hands in 'peace signs' for a second) "Some things are going to get easier. Some are going to get worse."

Me: "Am I in a coma after all? Why does everything—or almost everything—seem so real? Your move."

R: "Number Seven retreats four and over three. I capture the Letter C. I have to warn you, Avery. The bindings that have held you captive have also held you together."

Me: "What are... you..."

I look down at the finished game. The only letters remaining spell EUPATRID, which makes no sense.

R: "You are waking up."

And so I did. I got out of bed. I went to the game, which was barely visible in the glare of the artificial light outside. It was as I had left it before going to sleep. All the pieces were on the board.

I went and found the deck of playing cards. Riffling through them, my eye was caught by the patterns on the back. Each card's back was subtly different. It was a marked deck, but the markings were not indicating the identity of the suit and number --they were spelling out very simple instructions for a completely different "game." I had not seen it at first because, well, why would I have? It was a code. A complex one. One that I probably would not have figured out within a year.

Unless I had already known it, way back when.

Nov. 17th, 2004 12:28 am Entry 69

I have yet to try out the new word. The reason for this is difficult to explain.

I just had a marathon mirror-gazing session. Not in the Temple, but in front of the table setting in the Mansion. A number of things occurred to me while I searched my image.

Perhaps it should have been obvious, but this mirror IS the "statue" for the Mansion. Whomever stands in front of it is the statue. I do not quite grasp what this means, yet. Like I know what any of the statues represent.

I went back to the library to do some research. It turns out I had indeed seen the word "Eupatrid" before now. It refers to a member of the hereditary aristocracy in ancient Athens. Curiouser and etceteras.

Headache has been intermittent, but strong. The muscles in my hands and arms feel strange for a minute after I first wake up. I do not need to be getting sick.

What the Hell was Raphael saying to me? If I somehow had a hand with these puzzles, why do I not remember this at all? Why can I not consciously decode the poker deck, yet I am somehow able to do so in my sleep? Of course, I do not really know if "EUPATRID" will work, but come on. Of course it will. I played the game/clue/code with an Old Testament being who says he is really me. Naturally it will work.

But if it does, what does that mean for the rest of his speech? "I have to warn you, Avery..." And why "...and, heaven help you, Michael..."? If these representations of archangels are just my subconscious mind, what do I have to fear from the Left Hand of God? And why is his statuette so pissed?

I am coming across as tongue-in-cheek, but I am serious. I don't like it. I am scared of losing what little has been "holding me together".

And Goddamn it, these headaches. I feel like shit.

Nov. 18th, 2004 05:25 pm Entry 70

I passed out after using the key. I hope this is not the start of a trend.

I popped into Aerie, which is what I am calling the cold mountainous area (the Church lives there). The transition was rough, though—painful pressure change, a stabbing sensation right in the middle of my forehead, strong vertigo followed by simply fainting. I scraped up my face a little thanks to falling on gritty stone. I have no good idea how long I was out, but I think no more than a half-minute.

It is still colder than a witch's teat, though (a phrase I first heard spoken by a mechanic when I was seven. I still remember my father looking askance at me when I first repeated it, mhrip). The air is so thin and dry I might as well be on Mars, it seems like; the moisture leaves my tongue almost instantly if I am panting with exertion.

No Church here, predictably. In fact, there is a disturbing lack of anything. No statue (!), no structure, nothing obviously man-made except for a hinged metal plate in the ground. Despite it having a handle I could only lift the thing about an inch until I rubbed some soap and spit on the hinges (I have taken to carrying soap from the Mansion for the morale boost). I think grit had taken its toll.

The Hole is underwhelming, to say the least. Water, but no food stores (damn it), some blankets, toilet paper and a small medical kit. There is just enough space to stretch out if I wanted to escape the cold that way, but it seems far too airtight for comfort. I would be terrified of falling asleep if I closed the hatch—if I left it open, it would nearly defeat the purpose of keeping warm.

No statue, no structures, no clues, no keyhole. I am not panicking, yet, but the sun is setting and I am debating about just how important "air" is, anyway.

Nov. 19th, 2004 10:30 am Entry 71

That was a rough night.

I was prepared to spend a long night tucked inside the Hole, but that was just short of an eternity. Not wishing to suffocate in my sleep, I used a small stone to prop open the hatch about 3/4 of an inch. Wrapped in blankets, fully dressed (sans shoes—I have rarely been able to sleep with shoes on) yet still freezing, I was just starting to doze when I heard a thump outside. Something heavy with more than two feet made a sound like a monstrous crow in the darkness. After a minute I then heard damp snuffling at the hatch, less than four feet above my head. I was thinking "this is why the hatch exists—to keep these things out!" when whatever it was hooked a claw into the crack made by the pebble and LIFTED THE LID.

It happened so suddenly that I did not even have a chance to yell out (read: scream like a girl) before the hatch fell with a bang, the pebble falling onto my head. A moment of irrational worry lifted immediately when I realized that I was now safe for the time being. Yes I might start running out of air, but I certainly was not going to be sleeping anytime soon, especially as I was still hearing (or imagined I was hearing) the creature padding about outside, no doubt wondering where that delightful smell of fresh meat went off to. I wrote earlier that I had seen strangely shaped things flying in the distance as I stood by the Church; I wonder if one of those was what had visited me.

Obviously, since I am still pressing pen to paper, I did not run out of air. It made sense that the designers had thought of that, though it was nothing I had wished to assume. In the morning, after fighting off the weird muscle fatigue that has been plaguing me recently, I found an air pipe at the back of the Hole.

I also found the keyhole. See, no reason to panic. It was not where I had failed to sleep, however.

After having eaten a scant breakfast in the anorexic light of early morning, I set out to search for an outhouse, latrine, pit or convenient grouping of boulders. Armed only with a roll of toilet paper (having left the shotgun back in the library) I navigated through several austere rock formations until I found a flat clearing dominated by a sundial.

As soon as I saw it I suspected it to be the "statue," for it was made from the same tawny stone as the priest in the Church. Perhaps five feet across, perfectly round and with a severe, surprisingly skinny gnomon, it silently indicated that it was just after seven o'clock. The hour lines were not the only markings on the dial. The very edge had numerous small lines cut into the rim, not unlike a quarter-dollar coin. Forgetting my earlier urgency, I circled the dial and counted. There were 365 marks, although how the shadow could possibly indicate the day of the year, I have no idea. It was interesting to understand that such a subtly, yet decidedly alien land had the same number of days. On the other hand, it has been apparent all along that each of these places' day/night cycles are in perfect sync, so it only makes what passes for sense.

The base of the sundial sported the cross-shaped keyhole I had been hoping for. Above that was a dedication, in English.

It read: "In memory of Foster C. Torres. 2/18/1955 - 2/12/1995".

You can be sure I will deconstruct poor Foster's name in as many ways as I can manage. In the meantime, however, since the keyhole worked just fine, I will have a warm bath.

Nov. 24th, 2004 11:58 pm Entry 72

I have not written anything in a while because there has been, embarrassingly, nothing to report until this evening.

I knocked my mushy brains out trying to come up with a way in which the inscription on the base of the sundial would reveal the answer. I should mention that it was hard to devote my full effort to the task when, each night, I kept expecting the angel Gabriel to sit down with me in a dream and literally spell everything out.

He must not have received that memo, however, so it was only yesterday that I honestly focused hard on the problem. It is amazing how lazy I became when I thought the solution would eventually be hand delivered.

I wonder why it has not been. If all the "angels" are me, am I only breaking the silence when my conscious mind needs help? If so, where was my subconscious when I was starving to death? Why now? I get that things are changing. But what things? Does it cost me something to allow myself this hidden knowledge? Why is the knowledge hidden?

That, I think, may be the root of it all. Is it that a large part of my mind has been

What, petrified? Encased? And is it self-imposed, or did someone do this to me? "Officer Pymander?" The group of executioners in the painting labeled "The Crime"? The woman in the painting?

It was while wallowing in this mire that I literally stumbled onto a major clue in this area. Deep in conflicting speculations, hovering near the sundial, I tripped over my own feet. Reaching out to catch myself, my hand grabbed the lip of the dial. It spun.

But more than that, much more than that, it was like a strobe light had gone off. I lay on the ground, shoulder hurting from the strain, and watched as the sun visibly ROSE from the east. This was unexpected, as at the time the sun was about an hour and a half from setting as I began my fall.

I have been experimenting. As I rotate the sundial (only the outer foot or so moves), a day passes for each notch on the rim. That is fast, considering as I noted there are 365 notches for every full turn. The dial will not turn beyond "today", but it is fine with going "backwards", then "forwards" until I get to "now" again. Changing the time here does not, I have found, change the time in any other area.

If I move it very slowly, I get to observe myself discovering the sundial.

Nov. 26th, 2004 11:56 pm Entry 73

I am in bed, in the Cave, squinting through the blinding light of two candles, enduring another headache. My whole face feels like it is swollen and pulsing. I think in some sense I am trying to hold in my brains.

My sense of humor stands wounded, but resolute.

I spent some time combing through the days as presented by the sundial. It was fascinating, of course; an enormous sense of power accompanied the slow turning of the wheel (and quick passage of the pale sun). However, I became increasingly troubled with a growing disassociation. I would stop the rotation only to experience a profound disconnect with the physicality of the land around me. The ground, the chill breeze groaning over the rocks, even the air I took into myself—all lost reality, as if everything would fizz and blink out like a television image if I made too sudden a movement. I imagined I could actually feel the fabric of the world brush and catch. This became deeply disquieting, considering my tenuous and arguable grasp of what has been "real" since that strange day in August. I found I had to mark where I was leaving off, set the wheel back to "zero" (today... now) and wait for my head to clear before continuing.

Still, this temporal searching bore some interesting fruit.

Highlight: I saw in broad daylight one of the large creatures that call this area home. I very much suspect it had been one of these that had clawed open the hatch as I lay huddled. If I were being generous, I would have dubbed the beast a "griffon," but it lost the resemblance to that noble myth the more I had studied it. Perfectly combine a wrinkled greyhound with the largest condor on earth, toast the skin with a blowtorch, then cover everything except the head and wicked claws with a sparse, yellow down—you would have a fierce, yet pathetic-looking predator that I am quite certain could eviscerate me with but a snarl and a cough.

The painstaking turn of the dial grew frustrating after a while. The monotony, coupled with the eerie disassociation, eventually turned an engaging curiosity into a labor. My mind wandered, then started actual thinking. I did the math in my head. I turned the wheel to what I figured was February 12, 1995.

I almost missed it, as I think I might have misfigured a leap day somewhere. But there he was: the elderly gentleman I had witnessed in the mirror inside the Temple. His head slightly lowered, he was gazing meaningfully at me. He held a beige plank of wood with the word RECUSANT burned into it.

Another figure walked into the clearing. My head exploded into a million actinic sparks. I collapsed and vomited. With an effort I can barely recall now, I turned the sundial about nine and a half times, until it stopped suddenly. Blinking back tears, I dialed the code for the Cave into the key, my head hurting so much I felt as though it were floating on a cushion of raw, liquid pain.

That was a day and a half ago. I have not been in bed the ENTIRE time since, but most of it. The headache vacillates between "grueling" and "nasty," but I am at the end of the worst of it.

I hope.

Nov. 29th, 2004 08:22 am Entry 74

Lying in an exhausted, aching sleep, I had another dream.

I was in a library—an Old World book depository with leather chairs cradling old men with their noses thrust into newspapers; shelving fifteen rows high; ladders on rollers; enormous tables with brass reading lamps—and I was looking for something.

It was clear I was growing frustrated with the search, although I did not actually realize the target of my hunt until I came upon a case of nothing but the O.E.D. A gentleman was standing before them, his back to me. He was gently thumbing through one of the volumes. When he turned, still holding the open book, it was then I recognized him as Gabriel.

His genial face housed a friendly expression nestled cozily within his curly red beard. A slightly pinched brow, though, bespoke of anxiety, I thought. He motioned for me to sit at a table made from more wood than a frigate.

"Do you remember places like this?" he asked, peering at my face closely.

"I suppose I must," I said dryly. "If you are here to clue me in on the next word, I beat you to it."

His expression was replaced with... well, not anger, but a complete loss of humor. He turned and said something that I quite forget, something about the old men reading papers. I turned to look at them, then started violently in my chair when I turned back to see Gabriel's eyes not a foot from mine.

"Your memory will be a long time returning, fully," he said. His breath smelled of dust and olives. "But for now there is something you must recall. You MUST." He sat back and closed the dictionary.

"Ex... ex..." I was trying to say 'excuse me?' but the word stuck badly. "I... I..." Frowning, I felt the headache intrude into my dreaming.

Gabriel stood, this time looking as tired a man as I felt.

"If you can't do it by the time you reach Michael," he said, "this whole ordeal might have been for absolutely nothing."

I woke up in the Cave, shaking, staring wide-eyed at the solid image of my mannequin trembling by the foot of the futon where I lay. One eye was completely free of his blindfold. It bore into me like a bloody stake, pinning me to the bed. Sweat ran down my sides.

The thing gave a terrified, wet cough; foamy spittle dripped from its lips onto the blanket. Then it melted into the air.

Later, hours later, not knowing what trial to expect, I dialed the next word into the key.

I am sitting cross-legged in a light woods flowing with birdsong, watching a largish gray squirrel watch me. The morning light is yellow-gold and rinsed with the freshest air. There is a statue, fortunately, but although I spent most of yesterday searching this open, airy forest, I can find no other sign that the hand of

Man has ever touched this place. Nevertheless, I am sure I am not alone. I am certain there is someone here who wishes me harm. I can see his white robes out of the corner of my vision.

The squirrel has gone about its business, convinced for the moment that I am no threat, leaving me in an idyllic wilderness that feels like nothing more or less than a last stand.

Forgive the blood on the page. My nose just spontaneously started dripping the stuff while I was thinking about how to start this entry. It took around ten minutes for it to stop, leaving my Abborazh shirt a mess.

My headache is never-ending. It has moved gradually to a wide swath behind my forehead. It still hurts a lot.

Worse, though, is that I can't keep

Nothing has happened, although that might be because I haven't slept in nearly two days. No dreams, no visitations, right? Retreating to the Cave or the Mansion doesn't help. I am almost constantly seeing bright purple flashes of light out of the corner of my vision hearing things seeing things even feeling things, like someone breathing down my neck.

Body cramping, stomach twisting into acidic little ball. I cant concentrate

Little later:

The statue is an interpretation of Lady Justice, made of expertly carved pine, with a steel sword loosely held point down in one hand and a steel balance held with the other. On one plate is a (carved wooden) ingot, the other has a wooden feather. She is wearing well-wrapped "cloth" and robes, covering her everywhere except her head and arms. She is, surprisingly, smiling. She is not blindfolded, thank God.

Later still: More blood.

Im falling apart, heart racing waiting for a divine retribution I don't deserve. for the sword to fall.

Sword

Dec. 1st, 2004 08:39 am Entry 76

After fifteen minutes of figuring out how it was affixed, I managed to remove the sword from the statue. It reminded me of trying to open a Chinese puzzle box: twist right, two twists left, lift, etc. I am sure I could not tell you how I did it.

It is heavy. I think it is a real sword. The pommel is inscribed COLLOGUE. Is that a place name? It does not look like a real word.

I'm seeing a snake right in front of me. it is slithering over my ankle as I write this, even though I don't feel it at all.

It's not there.

I reek. Smell like a sewer and... acetone? Why acetone?

Have to drag the sword. Muscle weakness comes and goes, not just in the morning. What is happening to me

dialed it into key now just got to try it. just try it.

Dec. 1st, 2004 09:13 am Entry 77

Im here. No statue. Hot, sticky, humid, lots of insects. I think.

Exhausting carrying the sword.

Okay, resting again.

Dec. 1st, 2004 09:45 am Entry 78

Top of a steep gorge, maybe two hundred feet up. Fresh breeze helps with the heat. Bitten all over.

This is it, I think.

I have come to a bridge—narrow, but sturdy-looking. I am not asleep, but Michael is out there, middle of the bridge, waiting for me. White robes, sword held at the ready, as easily as a bamboo pole. Waiting. While I sit here counting the minutes remaining in my life.

Tried to vomit, but nothing left. Hasn't been for a while now. Did not want to alarm you, whoever you are reading this, but you know me, don't write about it, doesn't exist.

Avery Alexander Myer.

Might as well get this over with. I'm going to leave the journal right here.

Adios.

robin Robinmysweetestmyloving
      Wonderfullaughingchild Im**sosorrysweetie**

please I am so sorryIloveyou

I missyousoMUCH WHY please GOD

WHY.

Robin it should have been me

Dec. 5th, 2004 03:02 am Entry 80

I do not remember writing the previous entry. I barely recognize my handwriting. I was tempted to rip out the whole page; might as well, I thought, I wasted so much paper writing it anyway.

I will leave it in, though. In case I forget again.

From the bottom of my soul, I am sorry I forgot how you lived and how your life ended, Robin Elizabeth Myer Prescott., msrip.

Not that I remember much, but what I have been allowed to recall over these last few, wretched days—it is so hard to say: either I have regained a few important pieces of my own mind, or I have slipped over the edge into blind psychosis.

Either way, I feel

I think I am slightly more whole.

Take the rest of this as the ravings of a man who has finally lost it if you must. I could blame no one for doing so.

After wrapping up this book in my bag and leaving it, I plodded onto the bridge, dragging the statue's sword behind me. Each step took a year to place in front of the other. My hallucinations expanded until they filled every sense I possessed, plus, in all seriousness, one or two I did not know I had.

The image of the Archangel Michael—standing impassively yet sword at the ready—grew larger, brighter and somehow as white as a snow field. At one point my mind supplied the brief, silent image of Gabriel floating far above the bridge, shouting without sound, but the vision was gone in an eyeblink.

As isolated as I have always been since arriving in this nightmare, I had never felt more alone than that very moment. A part of me gave up, then; inside me, something human—desiccated by my pain and disjunction—something crumbled that moment into grit and gray ash. "My" sword dropped from senseless fingers.

I expected raw contempt to cross Michael's face. Instead, he merely seemed to find something slightly distasteful, as if an exterminator had uncovered a few more roaches than he had anticipated.

Roughly (and I imagine I am filling some things in long after the fact), here was the exchange:

"Defend yourself, fool," said Michael. He raised his sword until the bright silver tip was level with my headache.

I must have stood mute for too long, as he flicked his wrist slightly, causing a bleeding cut just above the space between my eyes. Startled into motion, I scrabbled for the sword. Taking it in both hands, I swung the thing with all of my remaining strength. In hindsight, while I recall a serious effort, I bet to the warrior opposing me it was done in slow motion. In any case, he must have simply stepped back, then thrust his blade through my left hand with casual skill. Unable to hold the weapon with only one hand, it fell again, this time over the edge of the bridge.

I remember crying out in terrible anguish. I saw my soul flashing into the air before being caught by gravity and vanishing from my sight.

"It's over," Michael said in a voice so firm it could have supported the world. "Your life ends here."

My vision swimming with tears, I could only see two seconds in either direction. I shouted out my bewilderment and frustration in one formless word and leaped after the sword.

Here it gets really uncertain. As near as I can figure, my lower leg must have caught in two of the tight rope lines on the side of the simple, but well-made bridge. I can vaguely remember stopping abruptly, my chest hitting the bottom of the bridge's side.

What was probably only a few seconds later, something happened. I really do not know for sure what. It might be that, in disgust or in aid, the archangel severed one of the lines. It could be that everything on the bridge was a massive delusion and I myself tied a rope around my shin. Nothing seems likely to be true.

What I remember next, in any case, was returning to consciousness perhaps twenty feet from the ground, upside-down, hanging from one badly abused leg. The bridge was nearly 200 feet above me. The sword was sticking point-first into the ground below me. Right next to me, swinging gently in the breeze, was a statue.

And in that position, more or less, I remained.

For two days.

Dec. 7th, 2004 07:24 am Entry 81

What does one do when the memories that return to you are stranger than the fiction you were living?

Getting back to the ordeal on the bridge: I swung by one leg for a long, long time.

I had lost a fair amount of blood, I am sure, from the clean puncturing of my left hand. I felt as weak as a corpse, most of the time. My head filled with blood until it overflowed my nostrils and ran into my eyes. I had the profoundly disquieting sensation of slowly, but concretely dying.

Between bouts of unconsciousness and bizarre hallucinations, I observed the statue for this area. It was perhaps thirty feet away and almost level with me; only a few feet lower than where I came to rest. It was made of a light wood, probably pine, although in that humidity how it kept from disintegrating I have no idea. It was a man, naked except for some sort of wide bracelets and a tied loin cloth, hanging from both bound feet by a very long length of chain. As we both twirled slowly in the constant breeze I saw that his expression was ecstatic. His arms were out, his hands flat, as if he were in mid-dive. Except for the chain, I would say he was, what do they call it, "bungee jumping" or some such.

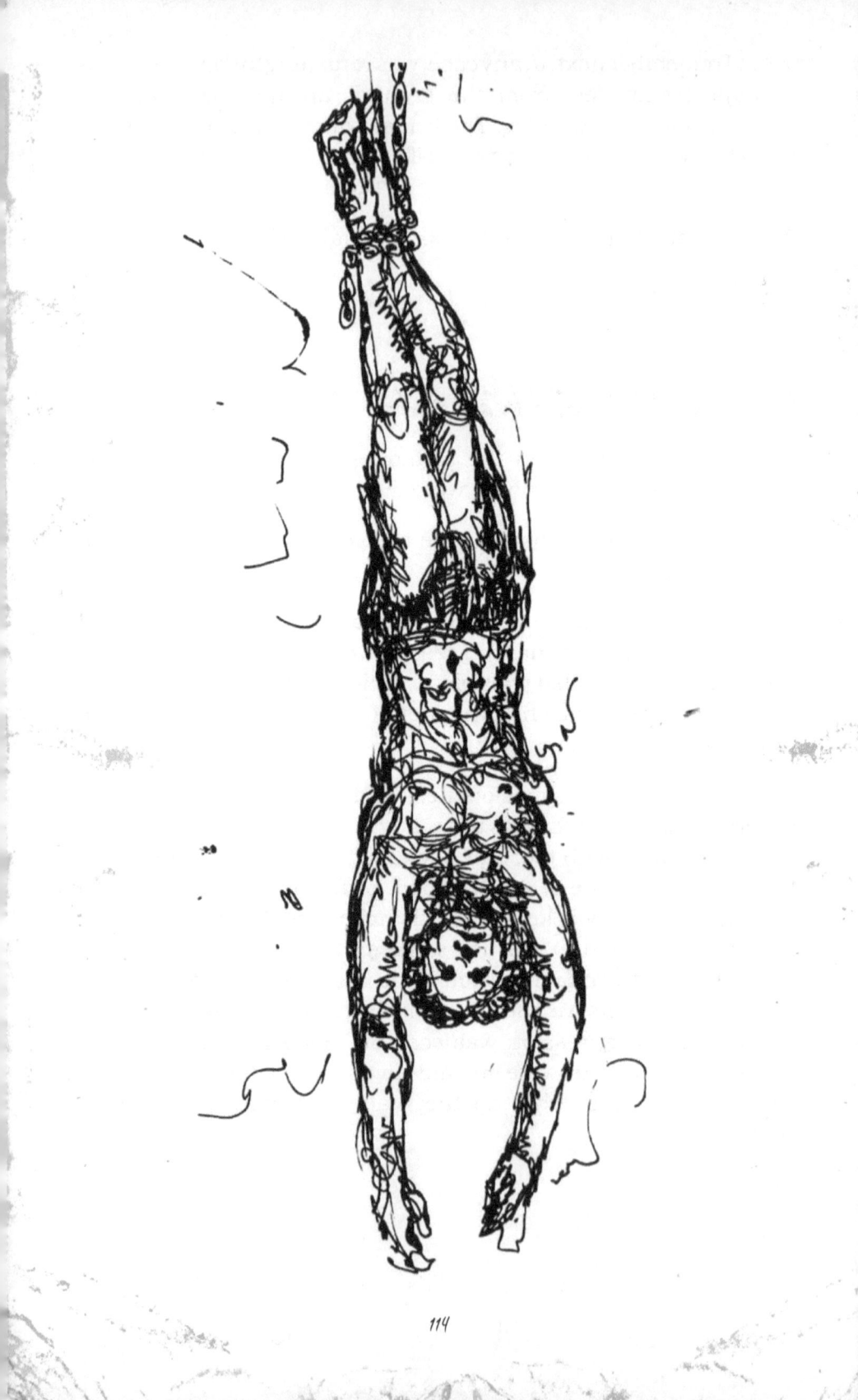

It took some effort, but I eventually followed the chain upwards with my eyes until I saw it was connected to the bottom of the bridge. Something else was on the bottom of the bridge, painted in huge letters.

ARTISTRY

Of this much I am reasonably certain. I can say that about nothing else, however. As before, I felt at times as if I had become wildly delirious. I offer no other explanation for much of what follows.

Certainly my bound twin made an appearance: I saw him on the ground, walking without impediment, blindfold hanging loosely around his neck. Ignoring me above him, he walked past the sword, giving it only a glance. He reached what I thought looked like a pale sleeping bag; I hadn't noticed it before. He stepped into it. Still standing, the bag enfolded him until it covered his head. After he was inside it completely, he looked—exactly the same. As if he had not put anything on at all.

Later, I recall shouting out in great anger. Every time my rage clawed its way out of my mouth, I would hear thunder.

Shortly after that it started to rain. I tasted the water as it filtered through my beard. I remembered the day when I was four and I had become separated from the church group as we hiked the Dakota Badlands. Not knowing better, I kept walking aimlessly, becoming more and more upset. In particular, I was very unhappy that I had to go to the bathroom, yet there were no bathrooms to be found. I was certain that just "going" on the ground was a bad thing. Half a day later, when I was found by an off-duty police officer, I had been so traumatized I was unable to urinate even when presented with a toilet.

That all flashed back into my memory when I realized that, hanging there as I was, urinating would be unwise. For a timeless moment, I became four years old again, in a very real sense. It is the only way to describe it; I began to seriously wonder where the group had disappeared to and why they had left me. The moment passed, but would return much later. More about that soon.

As time crawled on, I slipped further and further into a charcoal gray fog. My body had gone almost completely numb, which was both a terror and an enormous, blessed relief.

Gradually, I became aware of the oddest sensation. It felt like a hooked weight had been attached to a thread or web in my brain. As time oozed by, the weight was slowly tugging at this web, until it stretched past my skull without breaking. Longer and lower it stretched. The web entwined my brain, desperate not to let go. I understood then that it was alien; it did not belong there.

It had been PLACED there.

It approached the breaking point. Memories flooded my mind, REAL memories, the answers to everything that had been consuming me! I knew it all, the answers, why I was there, how I could leave, the nature of the beast in which I was dying.

The hook slipped, the weight dropped to the ground. With a moist, agonizing slap the web sprang back into my skull, sending shooting pains throughout my nervous system. I screamed until I tasted fresh blood. When I stopped to take a breath, I found I had landed almost head first upon the ground. Rain began to fall again; the sky above appeared swollen with water.

I cried. I had lost the answers when the web snapped back. I knew I had had them, and I knew they were still there, but I could not reach them. Or so I had thought at the time.

I now know that whatever happened to me, whether it was being so close to Death or the entire harrowing ordeal, whatever it was, it has left the web weaker. Frayed. Damaged.

I am beginning to remember.

What DOES one do?

Getting my strength back, eating, trying (with limited success) to gain some weight.

Continuing with my ordeal: I got rained on, that day, as I lay sprawled at the bottom of the gorge. I wandered in and out of consciousness, the pain returning in spades, as if it had merely gone on vacation and now found itself renewed and vigorous.

I am not sure what I would have done if I had taken the key out its accustomed pocket when I stored my supply bundle by the end of the bridge. Since the time I found practical clothes in the Installation, however, I have taken to carrying one bottle of water and the key on my person, rather than in my none-too-secure supply bundle. That day, as I struggled away from death, the precaution certainly paid off.

Unable to walk, I moved like a man twice my age. The pain was excruciating, but my spirit was still alive; it had dawned on me that, aside from a lump on my scalp from the fall, my head no longer hurt. My hand was pierced through, my leg was nearly black from bruises and constriction—but my headache was virtually absent.

Dialing the word, it occurred to me I did not know where the keyhole would be on a suspended statue. I remember moaning in despair, peering up into the spitting rain, wondering if I could somehow make it up there in my condition. Since I simply could not stand, I took that opportunity to search the ground just below the wooden figure. Fortunately, there it was, thank God. I brushed the dust and pebbles aside, slid the cover, inserted the key and pressed its button.

I arrived at the Playground.

More accurately, I appeared inside the odd little shelter that provides the "entrance" to the Playground. I should describe the shelter first.

It was made of brick, including the ceiling. The floor was dirt. The space was tiny, perhaps only as big as one of the rooms in the House. I mention the House, the first place I found in August, as it became clear as soon as had I tasted the air that I was back at the Seltzer Sea. The shelter had one glass-less window (very small, only a foot or so square) and an open entranceway (doorless). Bright sunlight entered through the door-sized gap, but was dimmed almost as soon as it crossed the threshold. This was not as oppressive as it reads—actually, it just made the outside all the more inviting.

Speaking of inviting, the only thing inside the shelter, besides me, was a statue. It was, appropriately, made of a solid white stone. A man was welcoming me to pass through the exit, his left arm outstretched, indicating the opening, his right passing in front of him to do the same. A very theatrical gesture. His hair was long and a little wild, ala Einstein, but with a clean-shaven face, big nose, slightly pointed chin. His clothing appeared to be fairly casual, with a broad, even exaggerated collar. His shoes had a bit of a heel to them. The only off-note to this eccentric, welcoming character was a "ring" on one of his hands—his left, according to my sketch—with a little human skull representation on it.

Start with a Berkeley liberal, add a cup of Willie Wonka and a teaspoon of Grim Reaper and I think that sums the thing.

A little giddy, I crawled out into the sunshine.

It has been an hour since I wrote the word "sunshine." I find it difficult to record the experience that concluded the ordeal at the Bridge. Not because it was horrible, or traumatic, exactly. In fact, it was one of the most wonderful things to have happened to me since

I entered a playground. A children's playground. And, as it seemed to be the law in that simple, grassy place, only children could play there.

This is so difficult. All manner of bizarre, weird, impossible things have happened to me here, yet I find that I am having trouble believing one of the grandest, happiest

Only children were allowed, so, quite against my will—for the span of an hour or so—I think I became a child.

At the very least, I distinctly remember the powerful sensation of the world growing huge and of stepping out of my enormous clothes and running, amazed and laughing, around on a lawn, naked in every sense of the word. I concede the probability that I am absolutely insane.

But when I came to my 53 year old senses, I discovered my body had healed, or mostly so, the injuries of the last week. My hand still hurt, but was no longer perforated; my leg was sore, but held my weight. I was still emaciated, yes, and dehydrated despite the rain and the long-emptied bottle of water, but I was— am—in one piece again.

After that, I eventually recovered my wits, dressed, and popped via the key back to the wilderness that led to the Bridge. The walk to where I had stowed this journal and my bundle was much shorter than I remembered.

I gazed out at the Bridge, now a blazing topaz in the light of a dying sunset. Michael was gone; there was no trace, save for a rope hanging haphazardly off the side. I crossed the Bridge, garnering no challenge. Red and yellow birds flew overhead. On the other side of the span, there were broken steps that once, probably years ago, had led down to the bottom of the gorge. Now it looked like the only way down was to climb the rope.

I sighed, ate every scrap of food I had left (plus some nuts I foraged), slept the sleep of the dead smack in the middle of the Bridge, got eaten by fewer insects than I had feared, and bravely made my way down the side. It was difficult, but for the first time in a while I had strength in my arms and legs. I made it without a hitch.

That more or less brings us to the Mansion, where I have been recuperating and bathing, writing and digging into a mind that is beginning to open like a winter crocus.

But that is a topic for another day.

Dec. 14th, 2004 02:43 am Entry 83

I am not exactly getting fat off of the Installation's food stores. This is at least partially because the majority of the richest food spoiled long ago. I did find a working freezer full of what probably was meat, but knowing the Installation like I do, I will not touch it much less eat it.

I have been hesitant to record my ruminations lately. As I stated before, so much of what is flowing out of my brain now seems

Well, seems nearly as unlikely as this bizarre, motley nightmare.

I actually went back into the Shack (during daylight hours, of course) and retrieved a few things, including the insect repellant as well as two more bottles of the sweet herbal liquor. Perhaps I am rationalizing, but a little high test booze might clear out some clogged pipes inside my head.

Anya, Erica and Nathan were real—ARE real people, compatriots, coconspirators. They were in the car with me. I was driving; it was my vehicle. We were getting the Hell out of Dodge, as it were. We had been found out, although by whom and for what crime

I am more than a little unclear. Far sooner than we had hoped, we began attracting police—or what looked like police.

People that were masquerading as police.

Apparently without cause, all four tires flattened and we trundled badly to a stop on a major highway. Debate quietly and quickly ensued. Were we going to fight? Run in four directions? Surrender?

No, it was decided. We were going to escape elsewhere.

Here. We were going to retreat to here. All of us.

It went wrong. Our avenue of escape was broken or destroyed by the "police." Only I made it, but not before something was deliberately done to my mind. It was not the translation to the Seltzer Sea that did it, of that I am nearly certain: it was an attack—a nasty mental or chemical assault, as weird in its own right as this conglomeration of worlds.

Whatever it was I had been brandishing—a playing card, my driver's license, an actual weapon—it is a key part to this fractured mystery, a piece I am having great difficulty retrieving.

I do recall one encouraging thing, though: the number of "worlds" here is finite. I am not sure how many, exactly, although I think I have been struggling to tell myself more about this place for weeks, now. There are some things the "angels" said that are growing stranger the more I try to make sense of them.

In any case, I have every reason to believe my time here is limited. The weight that removes from my spirit is tremendous.

I have much of my strength back. It is time to continue my journey.

I have got to get this written, or it will eat its way out of my skull.

Every area seems to have its unsettling element, as I have mentioned before. It would not have been my first guess that the most deeply disturbing would be of the Playground.

After my last entry, I waited until daybreak before I dialed in the word for the Playground. I studied the statue closely, in case I had missed anything previously. Aside from noting what probably was supposed to be a pocket watch chain, I saw nothing new, although it renewed my appreciation for the superb, markless stonework.

A memory is tugging at the bindings of my mind, suggesting that tools never HAVE touched the material in these statues. I have no idea what to make of that.

Anyway. I stood in the open entranceway, gazing into the already bright, slightly-off sunshine. I could just make out the peculiar sound of the Seltzer Sea beyond the walls that enclosed the Playground. The odor, the very feel of the air brought the strange water to my senses, as well.

What I could not do was step onto the grass. I am not saying, I do not think, that there had been a compelling force keeping me from doing so, although I will not swear to that; if it existed, it was subtle. Rather, I was struck with a profound respect for the magic of the place. Or, maybe, I was nervous that if I did enter the Playground, nothing would happen. No magic, no wonderful delusions, just a small, sunny lawn with two spring rockers, a sandbox, a brass rail fort and a tiny sheet metal merry-go-round.

It occurred to me the yard might lose that insubstantial sanctity at night. So, reluctantly, I backed away. Nodding to the statue, I dialed the Cave into the key and departed.

When I returned after dusk, I was met with a horror.

Brackish gray light flowed like a final breath out of the entrance, pooling around my legs and setting a chill so sharp it had been painful. I stared aghast at what used to be the Playground. I felt just the opposite effect from earlier: three steps forward before I knew I was walking, I shook my head and, with deliberate will, stopped myself. The statue, physically unchanged, grinned like a madman, cajoling me to pass the threshold. The odor of body rot sidled up to me.

I tore my eyes from the bone-white figure, past the gravestones jutting up from the blackened earth outside, across blissfully blank brickwork, then around and over to the small windowless hole.

Whatever it used to be, it stared right at me from the other side.

Complete. Silence.

Falling.

123

My heart stopped, perhaps literally. It felt like an empty, sucking void beneath my ribs for an eternal two seconds—then my blood unfroze, the air turned to shadow and I screamed. I screamed until my lungs bubbled.

I scrambled for the key, although I could not recall a single word to dial. I saw that it had fallen THREE INCHES outside the threshold, sinking very slowly into the crawling soil. I spastically groped for the thing with my left hand, only to pull back with a cry as blood flowed from my newly reopened puncture. I vaguely remember staring at my wound, then back at the key. Shifting my weight, I reached with my other hand, only to watch the key sink fully into the ground.

I dug at the earth as the flesh fell from my face.

When I awoke it was to that first pure, sunless light before dawn that seems softly crystalline. Key in my hand I lay dying, but confident that with the rising of the sun I would be largely whole again, and young. Before I lost my mind to the innocence that followed, I registered the word on the outer wall of the little brick shelter. Then once again I lost my clothing and watched with joy as the world grew big.

Later, with a peaceful sense of *deja vu* , I gathered my coverings in adult hands and departed. Not for the newly revealed area, but for the Cave where a bed awaited.

I slept the sleep of the living.

Dec. 23rd, 2004 01:47 pm Entry 85

Using cracker crumbs, water and some dried eggs I had recently discovered, I baked my own pan bread. My first try was disappointing, but I have become a little more skilled in the last couple of days. It is no less than ambrosia, particularly when it is still hot. It is a shame all of the vegetable oil I found at the Installation had been rancid.

In other culinary news, I have killed and cooked my first snake. I am here to report definitively that it did NOT taste like chicken. It was a bit like peppery frog's legs. Why did I wait so long to do this?

Everything I look at has taken on a different clarity, or some odd sort of depth I had not noticed before now. I will turn a corner and a scene I have witnessed a dozen times suddenly seems to be all "sharp edges and dewy color," to quote a publisher I used to know. It is like my surroundings have taken on an extra dimension; one I can perceive, but not identify.

Even stranger: stepping out of the Cave, I walked to where the statue was doing her usual fountain impression, only to see it had dried up. Or so I thought—a split second later my mind came to attention and all was as it had been. But for a moment—the merest jot of time—I saw only her dry breast; heard nothing but the wind and the sea. Then the water gurgled out of her white stone nipple as if it had never ceased, which I suppose it hadn't. I cannot reconcile the perceptions.

It has been some days since I dialed LANGUAGE into the key and appeared at the Blind. I feel quite secure there, in part because I am camouflaged, but I think the presence of a locking door somehow helps.

The Blind is in Aerie, so of course it is bitingly cold. The wooden building holds little heat, but there are several thick, warm blankets stored inside for which I have found myself enormously thankful. Still, it is a sturdy structure. Set on a cliff, the main part of it is literally built over a serious drop. The entrance is solidly on land, located within a crevice of the mountain. The lockable door is graced with a message painted in a delicate green: "Moderation in All Things". I can not decide if this is some sort of warning, or merely a questionable platitude.

The statue is several feet inside. Made of the expected reddish tan stone, it is of an older woman holding an object in each hand. Her haircut reminds me of a teacher I had in high school. Her gently lined face is bright with a sunny smirk, but her eyes are more serious. Her chin sports a dimple. She wears a floor-length skirt that ties at the waist, while a corset constricts her middle and covers her breasts. Her arms are bare, although one wrist looks like it sports a bracelet. Her armpits are unshaven.

As I mentioned, both hands are occupied: arms outstretched, the left one (her right) holds a featureless sphere the size of a grapefruit in her open palm. The other hand holds what I suppose is a long spear, except the weapon has an iron handguard. The spear is polished wood, tipped with brass—the only part of the statue not made of stone.

She stands in the center of the walkway, so one has to go around her to continue down the forty or so feet of carpeted (!) corridor. The carpet is berber, dirty gray and old, needing to be replaced. Just before entering the main room one passes a door to the right. This leads to a four by four room with a toilet, or rather a seat, a hinged pan and a pull chain. A canister of coarse powder rests 1/4 full, probably to be sprinkled into the pan for odor control.

The main room is the actual blind. Four horizontal windows, no more than two feet wide by four or five inches high, all exist at about chest level. There rests a wooden stool before each opening; two of the stools have three legs, two have four, if that means anything. Each window is covered with a hinged glass that can be raised and propped open. Outside the windows one can see a gauzy, tan drape. Presumably, this is camouflage to help mask the Blind from distant notice. It only slightly blocks sight from the inside, so one can observe the valley below almost as well as if the gauze were not there.

In addition to the blankets, there are two sets of sizable modern binoculars, two bipods to attach to the binoculars, several cases of freeze dried eggs, instant coffee, Tang and powdered milk. The only thing missing is water, which is an amazing oversight. I spent an hour just carting canisters of water in from the Installation, zapping back and forth via the key, driving my eardrums mad with the pressure changes.

I am making the effort because I want to spend more time here. Very little in the Blind suggests a clue for the next area. Believe me, I have tried—it's what I have been doing instead of writing in this journal. So I am going to camp out for a few straight days to see what, if anything, I am missing.

After all, these people were on the watch for something...

Dec. 24th, 2004 09:22 pm Entry 86

Not much to report. I am writing this by candlelight, drinking reconstituted (and cold) milk, huddled inside two thick, musty blankets—and bored to tears. Part of me is rethinking this "camping out in the Blind" idea that seemed so good when I was merely chilled, instead of blue with cold as now. I realize that having a light inside the Blind at night pretty much defeats the purpose, but I was getting restless doing nothing except wishing I could light a bonfire without burning the whole place to the ground.

The only thing to note is that this part of Aerie would make a heck of a tourist attraction for hikers and climbers. Scanning the environment with the binoculars, I noted several rock formations that would be a major draw back home, especially a wonderful balanced rock that looks bigger than a semi truck. Plus, the valley below—when it is not steeped in fog— is a shining jewel of verdancy.

After the night dropped like an anchor, I searched the land intently for any signs of fire or illumination. Neither candle nor lamp made a single spark in the wilderness below me. I suppose the solitude is oppressive, but I have become accustomed, I fear.

On that note, I record my official recognition that, if my own count has not gone completely south, tonight is Christmas Eve. If someone had told me in July where I would be and what I would be doing this Christmas, I would have clucked my tongue and peeled off a couple of twenties. There, but for the grace of God, I would have thought.

Ho ho ho.

Dec. 27th, 2004 07:13 pm Entry 87

I had grown weary of trying to weather the cold, dry reality of Aerie, so early yesterday I decided to abandon my camping experience in the Blind. I had gathered together the rations and equipment, setting them around the statue for convenience, when I took another long look at the sculpture.

I was fresh from viewing, once more, the rock formations outside the Blind, so it might have been those recent images that made that now familiar (and only slightly metaphorical) "click" occur within my mind. The statue held a sphere and a spear, or rather a spear with a handguard, i.e. a lance. A sphere and a lance. A ball and a lance. I remembered the precariously perched boulder so visible from the Blind.

I distinctly heard myself say "You have got to be kidding me." Ah, but it was only seven letters—maybe the rascals that had set all this up were not so perverse after all. Then I added a final "D" and shook my head. I half wanted it not to work. But of course it did.

BALANCED

I am beginning to miss those letter matrices.

So.

I find myself in what might be the executive offices of Hell. I am clearly in one of the upper floors of a high rise, as a picture window proudly peers over the same reddened wreck of a world that contains the Swamp. It is truly a land of nightmare, even from up here: a ruined downtown bathed in bloody light, cars charred or overturned, hardly a pane of glass intact on any structure—it is like a metropolitan DMZ. The ball of gore that barely lights the sky casts rusty, indistinct shadows everywhere.

I am writing this in a smallish, but richly appointed modern office, complete with computer and two desks. The theme is bizarre, though: "executive Goth" is the only way I can describe it succinctly. From the gooseneck lamp to the carpet, almost everything is black. What is not black is brushed steel, electric blue, crimson red or bone. In the latter case sometimes literally, as in a bit of "art" on the main desk that appears to be nothing more or less than a cat's skull mounted on a black metal stand.

The second desk is where I have chosen to write this entry, as the main desk is where the statue sits. Male, it is made of the same dark lacquered wood that characterize all the Swamp's statues. And, of all the statues in the Swamp, this one is perhaps the most thematically appropriate. He could be Satan himself as he would choose to appear on Earth. A lean man, he has a raptor's features: a hawk nose and an avaricious expression blooming from his eyes and engulfing the rest of his face. It probably would have been too much to have his hair slicked back, but instead it is an immaculate upper management cut, which also describes his (carved wooden) suit. His hands grip the front edge of his desk as in anticipation. His gaze is intent on the softly glowing, albeit blank, computer screen.

Yes, the screen was the only interior source of light when I popped into the room. I have since turned on a couple of lamps.

There is a locked exit to the rest of the floor, an elevator which lights up but does not seem to work, and a discreet emergency exit leading to a stairwell. This DOES open, although it is so poorly lit I have not found it necessary to risk injury just yet.

Although I may not need to, as someone has just knocked on that very door. Be right back.

I had a curious conversation with yet another part of me yesterday. Just as I think the most serious hallucinations have ceased, I find out they may have only begun.

I answered the respectful knock slowly, finishing my diary entry first, then stepping over to the recessed metal door tucked away next to a wooden filing cabinet.

"Yes?" I called out.

"Hello Avery," came a well-muffled voice. "May I come in, please?"

It was polite and it knew my name, so I figured it was pretty safe. It does not take much, around here. I opened the door.

Standing three feet away was the most handsome, nay, the most beautiful man I have ever seen. I consider myself unabashedly straight, despite (or largely because of) the weird, unhappy experimentation I engaged in my freshman year of high school. Having said that, I feel obligated to report here that something below the belt actually jumped when I set eyes on the man in front of me. When he smiled, I felt my breath catch.

Unsettled, I may have stepped backwards. In any case, he was too refined to obviously notice my reaction. He merely came inside the room, the light from the falling sun coloring his fair skin red.

Let me describe him: very blond hair sprouted off his head in every direction. The lines of his face were well-defined, masculine, yet his skin was so smooth and unblemished it still gave him a nebulous feminine cast. His right eyebrow was shaved off, his left was dyed black, which was not as bizarre and off-putting as it reads. At first I thought he was clean-shaven; it took me a minute into the conversation before I noticed an extremely light, wispy Vandyke. His eyes were a distracting pale blue, almost a colorless gray. He wore a chamois silk grenadine shirt that was clearly custom fit to his measurements, tucked into medium gray slacks. Boots and a belt as black as sin finished the ensemble. The nails of his left hand were painted black, as well.

He was taller than I by a head, but he did not lord that over me. Indeed, he seemed... not humble, but careful of my reactions.

"May I sit?" he asked.

I indicated a leather chair (black, of course). "Please do," I said, watching him closely.

He did so and so did I. He laced his hands together.

"Thank you, Avery."

"And you are?" I asked.

"Another part of you," he said. "I'm that part that is trying to remind you of your place in the world."

I am sure I blinked at that response. "In THIS world?"

He shifted his head side to side, his expression saying "Mmm... yes and no." He did not actually speak, however.

"Are you to PUT me in my place?" I asked.

"Absolutely not, Avery," he said intently, his eyes flashing. "Rather, I am here to elevate you. You have just started a very important climb upwards, by your own strength."

"Uh-huh." I leaned back, determined not to be fooled by the seeming reality of all this. I dared not treat it as an actual, normal conversation. I was, after all, supposedly talking to myself.

"You have a prodigious will," he continued, leaning forward slightly. "What had been done to you could not contain such a will as yours, not for long."

"What HAD been done to me?"

He gave a lopsided smile. "My principle purpose here is to tell you that you have some control over the reality in which you find yourself encased."

A silence gusted about the room.

"Is that because," I hazarded quietly, "this reality is all in my head?"

He sat back, as if unsure how to answer that. Eventually he spoke. "Nothing I can say will serve to completely disabuse you of the notion that you are actually lying on a table, somewhere, stuck inside a coma." The right corner of his mouth quirked upwards when he saw my frown. "In fact, Avery, what I hope to make you understand will probably only reinforce that illusion."

I took careful note of his phrasing.

I said, "I notice I do not have to be dreaming anymore to have these encounters."

"Oh, you're still dreaming," he said flatly.

I did not know how to reply to that.

He indicated my journal, still lying open on the smaller desk. "You should read through that," he said. "From the beginning."

"Why?" I asked.

"It will help my case," he said.

"Your case," I repeated, attempting to apprehend. "You are trying to prove...?"

"Your power," he said, rising from the chair. I found myself standing, as well. "Your control," he continued. "Your place in the world." He pointed to a deck of cards resting on a black shelf. He tapped them lightly, then turned to leave.

"Wait," I said, surprising myself. "I don't understand."

What happened next took a mere second of time, but seemed to stretch into a minute of sluggish motion—he whirled in mid-step, the back of his hand striking me hard across the cheek. My head snapped back and I lost my balance. The carpet took a long time to reach me. During that pregnant moment, I saw the stranger evaporate.

When time returned to normal, I was on my back, eyes watering, staring at the ceiling. My emotions were mercurial, liquid, trying to find a level. As I struggled to sit up, they settled on anger.

Clenching my teeth, I stood; I could not tell if the red of the room was from the sunlight or my rising fury. I saw the poker deck on the shelf, still wrapped in its plastic. I grabbed for it and threw it in mad frustration across the office.

Whereupon the deck burst into livid orange flame and disintegrated before hitting the opposite wall.

I felt the heat on my face. I heard the whoosh of the abused air. I could smell—can STILL smell—the acrid ash of the plastic coated paper.

More than anything, though, was the feeling of a living force as it had left my body and, in a rage, destroyed the deck of cards.

I took his advice. I reread this journal, from my disturbingly upset scrawls to now.

It is as if I had found the diary of a distant friend, in some ways. I only vaguely recall writing that first entry. I winced at how rattled, yet conversational I was. I had been groping at anything to restore normalcy, without understanding that what I was reaching for was even further from whom I really am. I remember it took about a half-hour to write the whole thing; for some reason, that was important to me at the time. I do not recall falling asleep mid-word.

The handwriting gives me chills.

Later on, the most profoundly disquieting aspect was reading and reliving my delusions concerning my daughter, msrip. If I had been so mentally wounded as to forget she had died, much less HOW she had died... I sit here wondering with a faint, pallid horror as to what even now could be missing from my memory. It brings to the front something that has been running through this rapidly filling journal from nearly the beginning: how much of who I am—who any of us are—is defined solely by those dubious truths we can recall?

It is no wonder my mind has split in order to reform. I saw those statues in the library of Abborazh and something inside my brain latched almost instantly to the imagery, the mythology of the Archangels. They became the icons for my reconstitution.

That does not, however, explain my most recent visitor.

Certainly I have no conscious memory of having seen the man before. It did not escape my attention, even during his visit, that he had avoided identifying himself. If we were going to continue the Archangel thread, he might represent Samael or some such. But I do not think so.

As for my display of numinous combustion: let it suffice to say, for now, that I have not been able to repeat the event.

I have been meditating recently. It was something I used to do, I believe.

When I am not doing that, I am trying to find the word to proceed to the next place. I have an idea where to start—I only noticed an hour ago that the keyboard in front of the statue's computer has a decidedly nonstandard letter arrangement. It is not a QWERTY, it is an MXBVOH.

More news as events warrant.

Jan. 2nd, 2005 09:36 pm Entry 90

I was meditating in the Cave—which has become my favorite spot to regroup, relax and self-explore—when I had an odd thing happen.

Actually, I should back up a bit: lately, as I meditate, I have the sensation of seeing while having my eyes closed. I am not sure WHAT I am seeing; it is not a literal image, much less one of reality (whatever that means, here). Instead, I get the profound sensation of visual perception without actual sight.

The closest thing I can compare it to are those rare times I have been awakened in the middle of the night, knowing somehow that what brought me out of sleep was a noise, even though I could not tell you what it had sounded like.

This is the same thing, roughly, except as a continuous experience.

As to the "odd thing" above, it occurred just last night. Thoughts drifted through my mind without settling or even leaving much of a mark. I had just begun experiencing the "sight without sight" phenomenon, when I noticed a nebulous pressure building around me. I "saw" this pressure, this increase in formless reality, without having it register as light or color (having written that, I need to add that I got an impression that I can only describe as "silver" or "shiny gray"—I know, it is a contradiction that I cannot resolve). It was not flowing from myself, but in most ways purely external. In fact, I got the distinct impression that it was trying to enter my space. Not in any way feeling threatened, I allowed this.

Since having done so, even as I write this now, I feel different. I am fuller, in some way, without any recognizable sensation of internal pressure. Not just that: places and objects that I have looked at and even studied closely now appear subtly different, in a way I simply can not put down on paper.

Did something alien enter? I am not sure, but it does not seem like I have "somebody else" within me. I feel exactly like I had previously, except... more so?

After hours of experimentation on the keyboard in the Executive Office, I thought to type the name ABBORAZH into it, but pressing the keys as if the letters were in the traditional QWERTY arrangement. What pops out on the screen, but SOOTHSAY. Okay, I will confess it: that is a clever way to present a substitution cipher. I just wish I had thought of it three hours ago. This place unnerves me, making me increasingly jumpy. It really does have a generous taste of Hell about it.

But was the code done after the fact? What I am asking is which came first, the code, or Abborazh? Did whomever was responsible for this motley collection of worlds sew a zillion company shirts with the fake name Abborazh JUST SO some fool would come by and discover the key word for another area? If not, was it just lucky chance that one could do a direct letter substitution for a fairly appropriate English word like "soothsay?"

The question of just who (and what!) these people are has become more and more relevant now that I am pretty sure I am one of them. Do I have, locked away in what I blithely call my mind, some special management-level keyword that can simply zap me to the executive washroom? Or to the employee lounge? "Where have YOU been," they will all inquire, putting down their National Geographics, stubbing out their cigarettes, finishing off their cans of Coke. "We were beginning to worry."

For God's sake, is there a word to leave this place altogether?

On the other hand, according to some of my recently acquired memories, I left the real world being hounded by enemies. They left me mnemonically crippled, perhaps to make me more pliable as a prisoner.

When I do make it back, will they be there?

Waiting?

Jan. 10th, 2005 06:19 am Entry 91

I am changing. It is no longer a matter of memories reshaping my identity; I am starting to wonder—even as my thoughts dry upon this paper—if what I am becoming is strictly human. I have been in a wide daze all this week. A different reality has emerged upon the more familiar one. Like a time-lapse film of an uncoiling fern, a second universe, natural yet strangely foreign, has unfolded around me.

It now lies like a silver film over the worlds I have become accustomed to, revealing unexpected details—peculiar patterns, unusual congruencies and emotional energies—that have roughly taken my attention until I could do nothing but walk and stare, stare and walk, moving from world to world in a bizarre trek of rediscovery.

I imagine it must be analogous to the fact that flowers sport radically different details when viewed in ultraviolet light. I can now imagine what that first scientist must have felt like after such a disclosure: examining slowly at first, then frantically, racing from bloom to bloom, amazed at the changes, yes, the new patterns, certainly, but even more affecting would have been the profound apprehension that birds and insects live in an almost literal parallel universe; a reality, just as meaningful and rich, yet utterly independent of human perception. What a mindblower that must have been, yes? Imagine—coming to understand that there might be MORE such "realities" just a perception's twitch away, exactly as real as what we used to think of as "all there ever was."

In my new perception, nothing is exactly the same as it used to be, but most of the time the differences are minor to the point of being subliminal. There have been, however, some substantial discoveries.

For instance, I have since learned that the Mansion does, indeed, have an external doorway. I found it four days ago. It can not be located by sight, even if one knew where to look. Instead, as I paced the halls like a root farmer in the Louvre, I came upon a wall I had observed a hundred times before, except now the wall felt like a doorway. Not "felt" as in touch, nor did I quite see the difference. And the word was not "doorway," either, so much as "exit." But there it was, and I used it to leave the building I thought could not be left.

It is difficult to explain.

Often, these perceptions take on the semblance of concepts and emotions. The Shack was dotted with splotches of "Pain," for example—some recent, some much less vivid. They felt like sandpaper and smelled of cooked mustard. Except, of course, they neither felt like anything nor carried any odor.

It seems real, all of it. And it... everything... is seeming more real, more tangible, each and every day. I can almost reach out and grab a piece of reality, then expect to take away a chunk of it in my bare hand. Almost.

This is not insanity. I have been insane. This is not it.

Whatever governor was installed on my mind is rusting; dropping screws right and left. I can see its gears grinding smooth.

I am finished with revisitations for now. Time to move forward.

Jan. 11th, 2005 11:58 pm Entry 92

I arrived in a pyramid-shaped room—four sloped walls came to a point overhead. Each brilliantly white wall had a glass window letting in sunlight, which flowed generously into the small space. A very sturdy-looking wooden ladder led down through a square hole in the floor, directly in the center. The light-colored ladder seemed as if it had been carved from a single piece of wood.

Three of the walls and part of the fourth were equipped with a waist-high shelf. In the gap where the shelf was not, a tall apothecary chest stood like a man of many pockets. Inside the drawers and scattered about the shelves were numerous examples of the crafter's trade: a straight peen hammer, brass nails, iron nails and brads, a beautiful T-square, a carpenter's pencil, an interestingly baroque hand plane, a coping saw and other such things. There were no power tools.

In addition, there were simple, yet inexplicable diagrams carefully drafted on clean, small pieces of paper. The formulae and drawings nibbled at the back of my head, seemingly familiar without quite being so. Using my newly acquired second sight, I thought I saw patterns of "Purpose" and "Misdirection." Feelings of actual use (to craft wood or other materials) were very faint, often nonexistent.

After having peered out of each window in turn, I saw I was on an island or peninsula in the Seltzer Sea. I was also about eighty or ninety feet up in the air.

Touching the walls, I made the connection: they were constructed of the same salt-like stone as the Sea's statues. I wondered, was I actually INSIDE the statue of this ca

I almost wrote

Hell and Damnation! Why did it TAKE me so long?

No, I know the answer—it must have been one of the things on which my attackers had concentrated, like obliterating my ability to read Latin, or to "see" in the manner I had recently rediscovered. They did not want me to make the connection. Or, more likely, they had wanted to keep me from escaping, except they had been just a split-second too late. Instead, all they had done was to prevent me from understanding where the Hell I was—AFTER I had arrived.

Well well well.

At least now I know how many more of these worlds I will have to travel before I reach the end.

Jan. 12th, 2005 10:47 pm Entry 93

I had finished exploring the Tower, still unable to find the next word. Just as I had settled down to write my observations, who should walk into my field of vision but the stunning blonde from two weeks ago.

Roughly, this was our conversation:

"So you figured it out, eh?" he said. His face carried a smirk so light I nearly missed it, but his tone was otherwise serious.

"Yes," I sighed. "I seem to be trapped in a Tarot deck."

"Took you long enough."

I felt my face go red. "You could have told me!"

"I'm YOU, remember?" he scolded, gesturing with a manicured hand. "We've been trying to tell you for quite a little while, now."

I nodded, sensing the truth to his statement. I briefly reviewed my recent dreams. He was silent while I did this; silent, but watchful.

"What threw me," I said, "was the lack of a statue in the second area... the second card, I suppose."

"You were the statue, Avery," he said, his words soft and smoky, like a dying campfire. "The mirror was showing you, behind that table."

"That would make me the Magician."

"Yes," he agreed. "It would."

A long silence reigned. When I next spoke, my throat was dry.

"I... I don't feel like a normal person. In my recovery, it seems I have rapidly passed 'normal' and moved right into... I do not know what." I saw I had started to wring my hands. I let them drop.

"That is my function, Avery," he said. "It is my job to make sure you become the man you were before all of this happened."

"Just who ARE you?" I snapped, turning in my chair to face him.

"Again, I am YOU, Av..."

"I know that," I interrupted, scowling. "Damn it, I know that. What I meant is whom do you represent? You do not look like anybody I have ever known, that I can remember."

Black ire flashed behind his eyes for the barest moment, startling me. It was gone almost before it had stained the blue of his irises, however; his expression was now one of sincere concern.

"I am that part of you who wants to rise as far above a 'normal person' as you can possibly reach," he said slowly, gently. "You are so much more than that, SO much more. The everyday, normal person is a cipher compared to you, Avery. A sleeping animal, twitching in his own wastes."

I sat there, unmoving. Images of my daughter flew through my rolling mind. Of my parents. Mtrip.

"May they rest in peace," I whispered.

He looked puzzled.

I thought of Rubina. Of Marian, as the elevator doors closed before her. I shook my head.

"Just... get out." My words grated past a barren throat. "Leave me."

The expression drained out of his features. He did not become angry, or confused. A mask fell across his face, plain and invisible.

I stood abruptly, clenching my fists. "Get thee behind me," I growled.

He took in a deep breath, then nodded.

"I'll be back for you," he promised. "You are more than you think you are, whether you want to be or not."

And, just like that, he vanished.

Jan. 14th, 2005 07:00 pm Entry 94

The sands here do not jump with skittish worms, nor do the skies support majestic bats, but the tea-colored sea does hiss softly to itself. I must be many miles away from the House, the Cave, the Mansion... or should I start referring to them by their now-obvious designations: the Fool, the Empress, the Magician?

Miles away, yet clearly on the same world. It boggles me to think how large these alien environments must be. These are not amusement parks conjured for the frustration of those who journey through this damned Deck. These are real places enlisted to provide a backdrop to... whatever function the Deck serves.

I wish I knew the answer to that. I truly do. If I had to guess, it seems today to serve as a combination gauntlet and learning tool. Perhaps it thins out those prospective apprentices who wish to join. An entrance exam to beat all entrance exams.

I do remember that this wondrous Deck only contains the Major Arcana. This means there are twenty-two total "lessons" to this journey. What follows the Tower would be the Star, the Moon, the Sun, Judgment and the World. And that, as they say, should be that, assuming I do not recover enough memories to recall the keyword for "out" before then.

In any case, night is falling. The first stars bright enough to be seen through the sea haze are making their appearance. I am back inside the ground floor of the Tower—a structure rising out of the sand like the miniature ghost of the Washington Monument—with several candles flickering audibly in the steady draft. Since there is no discernible clue to the next keyword inside this structure, I had been combing the land around it for any trace of an answer, to no avail.

But I will find it. I know that, now. Avery Myer will make it out of here in one piece, I feel certain.

Just who Avery Myer will be when he does so, however... that, I fear, is the real question. For I lit those candles without matches. I traced a remembered pattern in the air and they lit.

Like magic.

Jan. 16th, 2005 03:15 am Entry 95

This is becoming ominous.

Twice, now, I have caught the blond man watching me from a distance. I do not get any sense of warning, no hairs rising off the back of my neck or feeling of "being watched". I simply spotted him once while scanning the horizon and once when looking out across the beach from the top floor of the Tower. He was just standing there, facing my direction, about as far away from me as he could have been and still be seen.

I disturbs me on general principle, but also for the fact that I do not get any dread feeling before it happens. That would be expected if it were another person, but the blond man—he's me. I should get some notice when my subconscious is trying to tell me something, yes?

This train of thought runs on some awfully dark tracks.

He IS me, right? Just one of many delusions working their way through my sabotaged mindscape. But, if he is not some mental goblin prancing about, well, who the Hell is he?

Did one of my enemies follow me here, after all? If they did, would I be able to tell? I never think to peer at him steadily with the "second sight" I seem to have developed, as his presence has been more than a little distracting, so far. I must remember to do so.

Along those lines, how does a mental construct smack you across the face so hard you fall? Or, worse, stab you through the hand with a sword, leaving a vivid pink scar?

It is usually around this time (far past midnight, far before dawn) that I revisit the unkillable notion that all this is a coma dream. Come dawn, though, it becomes too hard to believe, if only because everything—down to the strangest, most insane moment—is just so REAL. The cramp in my writing hand, the toothless whistle of the wind through the window panes, the sand still stuck between my toes, the odor of the candles, the sharp tang of the magic that lit them. Even that. As the sunlight calls the lie of night, such thoughts evaporate with the darkness. When they return the next night, they are that much weaker.

Because, really, how can anyone prove that ANY given moment is not a coma dream?

Jan. 18th, 2005 06:45 pm Entry 96

My madness not only has method in 't, but it can be a right bastard, too.

I was being driven to idiotic distraction by the intermittent appearance of the blond man. He would materialize off in the distance only often enough to keep me painfully alert. Then just yesterday he turned up immediately behind a door just as I had opened it, startling me so badly I dropped my plate of dinner (freshly cooked snake, milk pudding and foraged potato-like tubers—I have become much less reliant on the food stores of the Installation, lately). He instantly disappeared into the clear air. I thrashed around in a fury, then settled into a gritted paranoia such as I have rarely felt.

Which, it turns out, was exactly what "he" wanted.

I became more and more keyed up, wondering if my tormentor would be around the next corner, or the next. I alternated between trepidation and seething anger. It was during a bout of the latter when I felt my senses expand: not into some new dimension, as last time, but farther outward into this one.

Abruptly, I could almost literally see behind me, above me; when I concentrated, I could intimately sense every object and force in a bubble roughly twenty feet in diameter. If I do this while meditating, the bubble grows until I have the unique experience of perceiving an entire structure, without and within, all at once. The information gleaned in that manner is confusing at best, so far. More often it is overwhelming. Still, I am sure I will become accustomed to the ability. After all, it is an ability reclaimed, not discovered. Due to the blond man's machinations, I have taken another step further into my power; another step away from what I had been.

He had me read through this journal from the beginning, I think, to illustrate my transmogrification from a simple, scared man into a being capable of killing and cooking a serpent with a gesture and an exercise of will. But I wonder if it has worked too well.

I can, even now as I write this, feel the alien power writhing about inside of me. It seems foreign, I think, only because the damage done to my psyche had made me incapable of remembering it, much less controlling it. Nevertheless, foreign it is. I can sense myself changing daily, almost hourly, in a real and visceral fashion. The more I use my unearthed will, the more I become something which I had not been only weeks ago.

It is not comforting, not by any stretch of the word, to experience this. Ironic, I think, to find it easier to live a fiction than to alter fundamentally into a true person. Whoever (or whatever) that might be.

I actually miss the man who was starving to death. I find myself wishing I could go back to being the bookbinder who still had a breathing daughter. I miss her most of all.

When I was a child, I had a picture book of puzzles and illusions. Actually, I had numerous such books, as it was a simple fascination of mine, but one in particular stood out because of its plethora of anamorphic images. I had been given this book as a birthday gift, along with a polished cylinder of some inexpensive metal, which at the time confused me. I soon discovered, however, that inside the book were these strangely warped, nearly unrecognizable pictures. When I placed the cylinder end up at a certain spot on each image, a perfectly euclidean and proper painting or sketch was revealed on the surface of the tube.

Also contained within the book was the type of anamorphic where one had to hold the edge of the page right up to one's eye, thereby foreshortening otherwise severely elongated words and pictures. It was one of this kind that I had finally discovered on the Tower.

As I had written before, the Tower's statue—that is to say, the Tower itself—was made from the same salt-white stone as the other statues residing by the Seltzer Sea. What is barely remarkable is that on each of the four vertical surfaces of the Tower are numerous striations; grooves painted a dark gray that I had thought for the longest time were abstract ornamentations, at best. Turns out this is apparently true for three of the sides. The fourth, if I viewed it from the very bottom with my head pressed against the wall and my eyeline straight up, foreshortened into an eight-letter word in a block font.

UNFETTER

I wonder if that same picture book had inspired me to create this conundrum in the first place. It is a thought that turns my mind around mercilessly.

I have not seen hide nor hair of my blond proscience recently. I imagine his work is done, for the nonce. Time will tell how long that lasts.

I should probably explain. It is only courtesy to define words one has just made up: I have begun to think of the Blonde as that part of me that eggs me on to greater and grander immoderation. Sort of the opposite of a conscience, he is there to encourage my excesses. A proscience, therefor. I shall contact the O.E.D. when I get the next chance.

I used the key. It brought me to breezy, thorn-ridden hills throbbing with grasshoppers. The heat of sunset had that menacing quality that told me it was merely resting—it would be back tomorrow with a vengeance. Right then, though, it was tolerable, even comfortable. The air smelled of rain, but the skies were mostly clear. A quarter moon wandered low on the horizon. The whole place felt very Earth-like. Presumably, I had made it to The Star.

As the darkening sky bled from orange to that specific, amazing blue I have only otherwise found on the "high-beam" indicator in cars, I walked up the slope of the highest hill to meet the statue. She was dressed for the earlier heat of the day in shorts, a halter top, a broad-brimmed hat, rolled calf socks and hiking boots. She had hanging on her belt a (carved) case of the type that used to be more common in the 50's and 60's: she used a slide rule. A canteen was represented on her other hip. Extending her rear in a jaunty, yet unselfconscious manner, she peered intently, even happily, through an oddly stylized telescope constructed of the same iron and pine materials as the rest of the sculpture. The whole thing—the woman, the telescope's tripod—was mounted on a base rather more prominent than on most of the other statues.

The telescope was of the type where one looks into an eyepiece perpendicular to the main tube. A reflection telescope? I do not really know. In any case, it was pointed maybe 75 or 80 degrees off of the horizon, that is, closer to "straight up" than not.

I peered at the entirety with my second sight. Almost instantly, the form blossomed into strangely shaped colors: much of the statue went nearly black, but sported a cream-white aura of sorts that communicated concepts like "Purpose", "Communication" and "Misdirection." The telescope itself was vaguely salmon pink, while the slide rule case flashed with an uneven yellow fire, along with the quality of "Inconstancy."

Memories started to seep into my consciousness.

Looking up, the stars had begun to reveal themselves in their deepening perch. The sky was simultaneously foreign, yet familiar. Seconds later I realized I was gazing upon the star field of the Southern Hemisphere. I pondered for a moment the incongruity of recognizing this hemisphere, yet not remembering what kind of telescope the sculpture represented. Setting that aside, I studied the sky again, but it told me nothing else.

I reached for the slide rule case. More precisely, I pulled at the metal tab that would have been, on a real case, the actual rule. It slipped out, clearly designed to do just that. Eight tabs along its length—pieces of metal that did not belong on a slide rule—spelled out "nqilposf."

I am sure I must have blinked at it. The word "anagram" flitted out of my mind as soon as it had entered. There was no "u" for the "q", for one thing, most of the time a dead giveaway. And as I watched the letters, the statue swiveled ever so slightly on its base as a stiff breeze pressed through like an impatient traveler. As this occurred, the letters changed slightly, to "nqisposk". Intrigued, I pushed at the stargazer. This caused the whole thing to rotate several degrees. The letters on the rule changed so rapidly the click of each made a buzzing sound. It soon read "tnoxzaox".

Very interesting, I thought.

I looked back up at the sky. One star, less than a handspan away from directly overhead, stood out prominently. From the back of my brain I recognized it as Sirius.

I heard a "click." Curious, I checked the slide rule again. It read "vnoxwaox". I assumed it was the wind.

I rotated the statue until I had the direction of Sirius (if not the ascension) lined up with the 'scope as best as I could estimate. The rule read "nehtirte". As I watched, trying to figure out an anagram, the letters clicked: "nekfirte". I tapped the statue very lightly. Again, it read "nehtirte."

THIRTEEN.

The wind had not done it. It was the motion of the planet, somehow. The statue would only show the proper arrangement if it were pointed in the direction of the brightest star in the sky. How did it manage that? A computer and a complex gear mechanism in the base? Heaven help you if it were cloudy that day, I suppose!

So I dialed the word into the key, checked my belongings (which had not changed in the short time I had been there, but it was a good habit), inserted the key and off I went once again...

...to the most breathtakingly beautiful area I have ever witnessed. I have yet to explore it, although it was an effort not to do so as soon as I had arrived. I must have stood there, stunned, for minutes.

Now, however, it is time to put this pen down and get some sleep.

Jan. 23rd, 2005 04:00 am Entry 98

I write this scant hours after having committed a murder. For all that, I am so calm my body feels hollow.

Excuse the miniscule handwriting; I have so much to put into ink and I refuse to weigh every letter as it passes my pen. The existence of this journal has taken on a new meaning, of late. Or perhaps it returns to its original purpose.

I will continue where I had left off: the land I found myself in (was it really only three days ago?) was breathtaking. It appeared to be located in the same universe as the Temple, i.e. The Lovers; grand, sweeping exaggerations of Nature as far as the eye could see. After having reluctantly left to catch some sleep in the Cave, I arrived back in the new area only a minute after dawn. The sky had been a rich melange of colors radiating from a sun too big and saturated to be the one Earth possessed.

I was upon a sizable peninsula that extended forcefully into a lake of astounding blue. The land was a rolling jut of round, almost suggestive hills and hillocks. I stood at the base of the peninsula, on top of one of the taller prominences, side-by-side with the statue. The air was crisp with sound; a salad of distant lake water, plentiful birds and a fresh wind.

The statue stood silently, yet praised the skies with a religious fervor all the same. Another woman, this one looked about 80 if she were a day. She was made from green marble. Her hands were raised in celebration or impassioned supplication. Bangles, all carved from the same stone, seemed frozen in mid-dance about her arms. A somewhat ratty-edged robe ensured her modesty and sandals protected her feet. Her nails were long and a trifle wicked; a distant echo of a bear's claws. Her expression was a perfect mix of triumph, pleading and ecstasy.

The dawn broke onto the hilltops like a Flemish painting. It illuminated a solid stone keep squatting about a half-mile from where I stood. As I did not see any other buildings, I set off down the rather steep slope toward it.

The footing downhill was easier than I had anticipated, but the climb up to the keep was so vigorous I had to stop and rest four times, even in my new "roughing it" condition. It was nearly noon when I reached the fortification.

It sat like a stone tortoise, smaller up close than I had expected: a substantial wall twice my height made a secure rectangle around a tower perhaps forty feet tall. A gateway, however, stood open and free, allowing me easy entrance. Once inside, I saw three other blocky buildings, of which one was pressed up against the tower base.

Two of these houses were storerooms. This delighted me, as they were still nearly full of all sorts of useful things. Barrels of water, wine and pickled vegetables; yards of burlap, cord and leather strapping; carefully packed wheels of cheese, bags of black walnuts and sacks of salted rice. I half-expected to find racks of spears and wooden shields.

After breaking out, rinsing and making a meal of pickled beets (I looked like a particularly messy vampire afterward), I explored the tower and its attachment, the latter turning out to be a sleeping cabin, complete with bedding, mirror and wood burning stove.

The tower's entrance room was a cramped space good for little more than providing a spiral stair to the top. The stairs were of the kind that presumed no fear of heights, comprised as they were of nothing more than stones that stuck out of the inner wall. I ascended carefully.

Who should have met me at the top, but the Blonde. He reclined in a simple hardwood chair, his striking eyes studying my reaction. My pace stayed even as I made the last few steps, but I remember fighting my temper.

The top room felt surprisingly open, as nine sizable holes surrounded me and let in light as well as a fresh, moist breeze. The center of the circular room sported a modern field glass mounted on an aluminum tripod. The only other item of note in the room was the occupied chair.

"Merely two more cards after this one," he said softly, "and you graduate from your own school."

I gave a grunt, pretty certain I grasped the irony. I positioned myself behind the field glass and peered through the eyepiece.

His smile was almost audible. "Then, of course, all this fades away, leaving you... and your very real power... to do as you please in the real world."

Satisfied the instrument was not pointed at anything in particular, I slowly stepped around the tripod, scanning the landscape. "If that is true," I said, "why were there police chasing us? It did not seem as though I could 'do as I please' after..." I stopped abruptly.

There, standing a couple of hills over, was a tiny human figure. I could not make out much, but I could see that it was facing exactly in my direction. Not walking, merely standing and looking.

Suddenly, the Blonde bolted from the chair.

"No!" he cried in alarm. "No no no, not now, not him!" His voice carried back up to me even though in no time at all he was sprinting across the keep, racing towards the gateway.

To say I became curious is to make a profound understatement. This was my own mind acting this way! He knew what I had seen just as soon as I had spotted it. I peered through the field glass again.

Far faster than should have been possible (had he been an actual person), the Blonde had just about reached the other figure. I disengaged, checking the instrument for a "zoom" feature. I found a promising dial, so I looked through the eyepiece again, twisting the control. The image grew smaller, then much larger as I worked the adjustment. I saw a peculiar sight—a fragment of my own mind about to collide physically with another figure. I adjusted the focus

It was my doppelganger.

The one who had been bound until my hanging ordeal.

I watched, my breath like cotton in my lungs,
until the two figures met.

My head erupted in serrated pain.

I blacked out almost instantly.

My hand hurts, plus this place is as hot as its namesake.
More soon.

Jan. 24th, 2005 12:00 am Entry 99

I came to many hours after I had passed out so violently. I was still in the tower, but night had fallen deeply outside.

I lay there "counting my bones," as my father once remarked, mhrip. My skull carried an echo of pain, but for the most part I felt fairly well, save for a sore ear where it had collided with the stone floor.

Mentally, I seemed—I am not sure how to describe it. Perhaps "clear", in the same way a chunk of glass is clear. Thoughts just passed through without hindrance and little distortion, leaving few impressions or lasting traces.

I remember trying to summon the motivation to sit up. It occurred to me, quite abruptly, that as dark as the night sky appeared from where I lay, I could still see a ghostly white/

yellow light illuminating the stonework, the field glass, the chair (although the latter was largely in shadow). Curious, I carefully stood, prepared for a vertigo that did not occur.

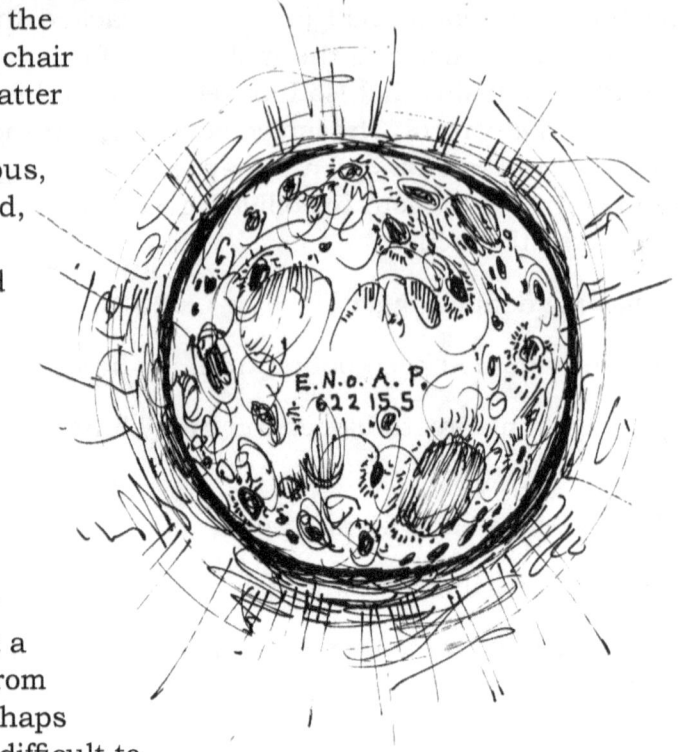

It could not be missed. Suspended by its own light, a beautiful "moon" hung in space at my eye level about a hundred feet from the tower—perhaps less, as it was difficult to judge scale. It could have been as large as four feet across. It was luminescent with an energy that did not fall into my eyes so much as enfold them; staring directly at it made my entire field of vision glow with its spectral radiance.

Setting aside the day's earlier events for the time being, I used the 'scope to look at the object in more detail. It was indeed a model of the Moon, including craters, seas and such. As my eye grew accustomed to the relative glare, I also made out some decidedly non-lunar details:

E. N. o. A. P.

62 2 15 5

I stood back, perplexed. Not so much because of the challenge it might have presented as a puzzle, but from the powerful sense of deja vu it triggered. I knew what those letters meant. I had seen them before; nay, I had created their sequence.

Then I laughed with the shock of recognition.

"Esoteric Numerology of Ancient Phoenicia"

A book in the library, back in the Installation (excuse me, back in "Strength"). A book that I had written, once upon a time. The clue referred to the 62nd page, 2nd column, 15th line down, 5th word. I chuckled, still bemused, even though it meant my trekking back to the statue to port over to the library and look up the word. Pity my returning memory was not THAT capable!

I left immediately, confident in my ability to navigate back to the statue in the very dim light. And so I did, only stumbling a couple of times, sensing neither hide nor metaphorical hair of my personal phantoms along the way.

The word is INFINITY.

I dialed it into the Strength statue and appeared instantly into the Sun card...

...and right in the middle of a life or death struggle.

Jan. 24th, 2005 03:17 am Entry 100

I had to get out of that heat. It reminded me of the months I spent in Atlanta; my brain simmering until everything I tried to write seemed no more than a damp white collection of foreign syllables. Air conditioning was not an easy option for me at that time. Fortunately such is not the case today, not when I can transport myself so effortlessly between climes.

So, to continue where I had left off, I materialized into a struggle as heated as the air.

The two combatants in the center of the stone room were literally at each others' throats: the Blonde, his features an intense mask of desperate hatred, was simultaneously trying to strangle and overbalance his opponent, the Doppelganger. The latter looked enough like me that seeing him in the physical grip of a murderous rage had me shocked to my core.

Surrounding them at what I could only describe as a respectful distance were the four Archangel/phantasms I had encountered previously. Their interest in the fight before them appeared to range from the casual to the captivated.

The arena was blazing with light so fierce, so sharp, the shadows cast could have cut skin. It coruscated from an archway set into the wall to the right of me. Above the archway was carved a sentence in Greek.

I yelled in surprise, trying to take everything in at once, then retreated from the fighters until my back met with the scorching wall. The combatants appeared real as real could be, but the Archangels had noticeably less substance to them, though they seemed not to mind. Their reality was hazy, as if viewed through eyes still half-asleep.

The Blonde thrust his opponent to its knees. Rage did not detract from his supernatural beauty even slightly, but the edge of desperation cast an unnatural, alien shade upon his face. It was briefly replaced with surprise when the Doppelganger swept his feet out from underneath him.

The intense wrestling match escalated into a vicious brawl. Blood started to flow as fists cracked bone with startling force. The match was not one-sided, but the Blonde clearly had the upper hand.

Inside my skull, I could feel my mind splintering with each landed blow. If the visceral analogy before me was truly such, the fight was a metaphor for the warring of fragments within my abused brain. The Blonde, I believed, represented an arrogant will to not only survive, but come fully into power.

Of my Doppelganger, I had no idea. But it was losing. I could feel it, even as I watched its flesh turn black with blood. It was dying.

The thought of a piece of me dying forever was intolerable. Becoming the Blonde, giving him full reign, scared me: his cavalier disregard for the people around me, those I cared about...

I hated that person.

I shouted for him to stop. My words seemed to stick to the very air, thick as it was with the heat. Still, he heard me, as he cast his blazing eyes in my direction. His features twisted into a sneer.

He leveled a brutal kick into his opponent's midsection and laughed. And as he won, I myself felt more arrogant, thicker-skinned, more powerful. I turned to my left, where Michael stood in his white robes. The angel looked impassively back, but his right hand reached for the hilt of his sword.

Suddenly filled with purpose, I strode over to the Holy General. He drew his weapon instantly, but instead of brandishing it he flipped it until he was holding the silver blade. Our eyes locked for a split second. Without a blink or contrary expression, the Archangel Michael gave me his sword.

I turned and advanced upon the Blonde. His astonishment erased all other expression.

"What are you doing?" he screamed, his bloodied opponent forgotten.

"I will not become you," I said. I gripped the hilt with both hands.

"You fool," he spat, backing away not one inch. "You ARE me!"

I raised the sword over my head, but it was not until it burst into a searing white flame that the Blonde finally displayed his fear.

"You cannot do this," he said in a much quieter voice, just before his head split in two.

As did mine.

Jan. 24th, 2005 06:01 am Entry 101

I awoke from unconsciousness for the second time that day. This time, I was in a sitting position, sweat dripping liberally from every square inch of my skin.

My double lay almost in front of me, horrible bruises blossoming from his broken skin. His chest rose and fell with a slow trepidation. Of the Blonde there was no sign, not even blood, nor was there any trace of the spectators. Michael had reclaimed his sword before leaving, it seemed.

My memory is a little hazy here, despite the events in question only being a few hours old: I recall trying to cradle the wounded figure, the apparition; briefly overcome with sadness, I left a suddenly empty stone room to climb a set of stairs; finding myself in a dark glass dome, I deflated where I stood and succumbed to a numb stupor. My mind was a shaken snow globe. I knelt dumbly under the dome waiting for the little silver flakes of my personality to settle.

This must only have lasted for a few minutes, although it seemed much longer.

When I stood up again, I felt profoundly different, but in a way I have just spent half an hour fruitlessly trying to convey on this page. I did not feel empty, nor was I wading in a dark melancholy. I did not understand the disappearance of the Doppelganger from my arms—was he "dead"? I could not detect any new gaps. Did the illusion merely fade once the drama played out in full? What did he represent, anyway, that the Blonde was so opposed to him?

I hope I have not acted hastily.

That takes me up to the present, minus the day to collect myself, find lots of water to drink and write this all down. The Dome is actually composed of sheets of smoky mica, not glass. When I first stumbled into it, it was just before dawn. After only ten minutes under the sun, however, it became as much of an oven as the room with the archway. This building stands in the middle of a desert, judging from the endless tracks of sand I can see beyond. Leftover mica sheets were on the floor in fairly neat stacks; fragments of stonework were scattered around rather less tidily. The air smelled of baked dust.

The keyhole was downstairs right next to the archway, where it must have been around 120 degrees. I could not read the Greek words above the arch (although I think I recognized "axios" as "worthwhile" or something close to that), so I am going to have to go back to the library at Abborazh to do some research. I suspect the clue to the next word depends on the translation. I hope so, anyway, as I have no idea where else it might be.

I killed a piece of myself. Sitting here in the gentle quiet of the Cave I can barely believe what I have done. It feels like it must have happened to somebody else. More than anything I remember experiencing such profound hatred. I did not even hesitate. I attacked with the intent to destroy. I hated him.

He was a part of me. What does that say?

Jan. 25th, 2005 08:52 am Entry 102

I have been reading back over my last few entries, having made an interesting discovery. After January 12th my recorded times started to fall regularly into quarter-hour blocks. I had not been aware of doing this, consciously, but thinking back I do recall checking my watch carefully and waiting for the "right time" to start writing. Then, several hours after the Blonde's passing, my entries went back to their more typical any-minute-will-do pattern. Or, rather, lack of a pattern.

I wonder which way was normal for me.

I had a striking dream last night: I was in a forest, walking briskly as if traveling with a purpose. I looked down to see a feathered arrow sticking out of my chest, although its presence neither bothered nor pained me. I came upon a cabin, the sight of which sent a tremor into my heart. Before I could approach (or turn away from) it, I heard a noise that sounded like a voice behind my back. I twisted in place, suddenly finding myself in the middle of a freeway. The police officer that has become a recurring element in my dreams these last months was there, drawing and aiming a pistol at me. On cue, I raised a card—now clearly The Fool from a Tarot deck—which exploded in my hand. Instantly I was back in the woods as before, but now the officer was with me. He (she?) started to glow with a golden/blue light, then transformed into a vaguely Vishnu-esque figure, complete with more arms than possessed by the average uniformed civil servant.

I am being flip, but the vision filled me with a dysphoria that pursued me into the waking world. It was a fantastic image that for some reason left me barren.

The Greek over the arch translated to "The search for real worth will consume all but the most deserving," or something to that effect. The answer was immaterial (except as pithy wisdom), however, as I discovered that the next keyword had nothing to do with it after all.

Thinking to use my extended senses, I received strong impressions of "revelation" from within the fiery archway itself. That left me briefly bewildered: was I expected to walk INSIDE that furnace?

To test a possible illusion, I tossed a scrap of rag I used as a washcloth into the "statue" of the Sun. It combusted so quickly it barely left a trace of smoke. Mmm-hmmm.

I am happy to say that coming up with the solution took me little time. I went into the Dome, nabbed a sheet of the mica, came back downstairs into the merciless heat and peered through it.

Sure enough, once the glare had been removed by the darkly transparent stone: CATALYST.

I popped into the Installation, gathered additional supplies and sat down in the library to write this entry. Now I am ready. Next stop—Judgment.

The penultimate card.

Jan. 26th, 2005 08:20 pm Entry 103

I am writing while waiting for water to boil. I am going to sterilize some makeshift bandages in order to dress a scrape on my knee.

I have been rereading the words of "Raphael" from November 15th: "I have to warn you, Avery. The bindings that have held you captive have also held you together."

That alarmed me at the time, to be sure, but now I am wondering what was really meant. My journey throughout this damned theater has coincided, perhaps not coincidentally, with my approach to a truth that has always been before me. Today I touched the few threads that remain between my mind and this truth and have found them very, very thin indeed. They could snap at any moment.

I sit here, waiting for a kettle of cotton stew to bubble, and I think.

Just what HAD been the effect of the "policeman's" weapon? I had described it previously as a web within which my mind, my authentic memories, were entrapped.

I wonder now if that is the entire truth.

Certainly the statue here, in Judgment, has started me to thinking; made from green marble, it is a precisely life-sized replica of me. Forget cleverly placed mirrors, this is the actual thing: a younger, cleaner, better-fed me, with the startling level of detail of which all the sculptures boast. Before him is a tall bench upon which a single-pan balance scale rests, as well as a large clarion. Everything is carved from deep-green stone.

I simply cannot get over how self-possessed he appears. I imagine I can even see a bit of the Blonde in him. For a while I just stood there, reaching out and touching my petrified image.

The centerpiece of this area is a yurt constructed with modern materials. It has been painted or stained with interesting spiral patterns, flowing in such a way as to seem to collect around,

on and over the single door. The yurt is situated in a clearing that appears too neat to be natural, yet everything is clearly under-maintained (read: abandoned). Outside the clearing are improbably prolific fruit trees, most especially pear, red apple and what I think are quince. Sizable birds that would be crows except for their white eyes and shockingly orange beaks natter about the grounds, pecking at the little black crickets which scurry everywhere. The breeze is fresh and deeply scented.

A weathered picnic table carved from rich brown wood stands by itself across the clearing from the domicile. The top of the table has a backgammon board painted on it.

Between the two is a well.

I always associate a well with my daughter, msrip. When she was seven and old enough to know better, she had been dared by a friend to climb into a dry well on the friend's parents' property. Robin, msrip, had been a tomboy through and through until she had reached her teens, when her rather explosive development into a woman put an abrupt stop to her more vigorous activities, for better or for worse. I imagine her male friends started to treat her very differently, as well.

Anyway, while the well here in Judgment did not look much like the one Robin had been trapped inside for thirty hours, I always think of her worried voice as it drifted plaintively up from the narrow, black depths. The memory cuts me to the quick. The water is boiling, but I will let it go for ten minutes to make sure everything is sterile.

I have been thinking of my girl Robin a great deal today, msrip. It wasn't until my ordeal on the bridge that I remembered how she had died, or even that she had. There is a part of me, small but vocal, that wishes I had been spared the reactivation of that memory. It is shameful to admit that. I value truth so much; plus, I am of the opinion that the deceased live on in our recollections of them, so to forget is the final nail in one's coffin.

But she had met such a wasteful, violent end. She had stopped by my home as it was being robbed in my absence. She either had let herself in with her own keys, or the door had already been unlocked—in either case, the burglars were caught by surprise and reacted brutally. Msrip.

This is giving me a headache. I am going to take care of this knee and continue writing about the well, later.

Jan. 26th, 2005 09:34 pm Entry 104

I am writing this with my double sitting across the fire from me. I had just finished bandaging my knee when he walked up as silent as a ghost and settled not ten feet away. Now he is just watching me, his lips soundlessly moving once in a while. He appears healthy and intent, not pained or even serious as most times before. The firelight flickering off of his face makes me dizzy and deepens my headache. I stood up to see if he would mirror me; he did, although not in perfect mimicry. Now I have sat down again... determinedly... to write.

The headache worries me. In the past headaches have been ominous. I have come to recognize them as having some connection with my memories or mental state. This one commenced during thoughts of Robin's murder. Although I have no idea if that means anything, at least it does not signal a horrible revelation. It does not get worse than outliving your own daughter.

Damn, but being watched while writing is really getting on my nerves, even if he is a figment of my bedeviled imagination. He is just staring and mumbling silently to himself. I think I can see the welts and scars where he had been bound.

Still, I prefer him to the Blonde.

I banged up my knee while recklessly climbing down the well. I determined it was dry and extremely deep by dropping stones into it. It was more like a mine shaft disguised as a well. I fetched some rope from the Installation, but ran out as I lowered myself. I still was not able to see the bottom, though that might just have been due to the lack of light. I laboriously made my way back up, bleeding from my knee. Now I am sterilizing some bandages I made from a uselessly worn shirt.

So, once I dress the wound, I am going to get more rope and continue my exped

Damnation. I had looked up only to see my Doppelganger sitting right next to me. It gave me such a start I inadvertently dropped this journal into the fire. I risked a serious burn getting the book out before any damage was done. Now he is gone. Christ. What the Hell was that about?

Damn this headache.

Jan. 28th, 2005 10:12 am Entry 105

It comes together.

I am all ready to proceed to The World; the last card in The Ivory Deck. However, I thought I would stop to put down what I have managed to digest since my second trip down the well. That, and this headache is causing my ears to ring.

Hidden below the ground here in Judgment is a museum, for lack of a better term; an informative collection describing the history and mission of a secret organization calling themselves The Society of Thoth. We, for I am a member, have subgroups placed around the world: groups with names like The Unkillable Idea, The Sublime Renegades, the Warriors of Isis...

I know. But, I have spent the last day or so poring wide-eyed over volumes of texts, modern and otherwise, describing in elaborate detail the machinations of this Society since before the 18th Century. There are scrapbooks so thick I can barely lift them, filled with newspaper clippings and well-preserved photographs of people and events so diverse that any common relationship does not seem possible. Yet, tome after tome describes in exquisite detail just how each thread of history has slid through the needle of this Society to some degree.

And the memories...! Even the photos that do not feature my (often significantly younger) face spark a section of my brain long thought dead to the world. I cannot go into detail, as it is called a "secret" organization for a reason, but it was exhilarating to witness large sections of my own life spread out before me. The politics we helped influence, the belief systems we steered, the private schools we carefully funded... the enemies we made; all cataloged for the initiate to discover when they had progressed this far into the Deck.

The Ivory Deck—a masterpiece of mystical redesign. The original had been called the Deck of Ninevah. It used to be a simple collection of five carved ivory slabs transformed by very old knowledge into a gateway into... well, no one is really clear whether they are "alternate dimensions" or alien worlds operating under unusual physics or magically created pocket realms. Some time not long after the Renaissance, the artifact was altered into the Major Arcana of a Tarot deck by chiefly European alchemists and craftsmen united under Egyptian mystical practices. Since that time it has passed from group to group, used as a hideout, stronghold, bivouac and, today, teaching tool for initiates into the Society.

Oh, God help me. I have used one of my last ten blank pages in this tired, travel-worn journal to catalog a library. I suppose I am trying to preserve my past and my current ordeal into the only "mind" I can rely on anymore. But, to know who one is— that treasure is beyond value. I would have danced around the entire time I was in the museum if I could have done so and read simultaneously. It was enough to make me forget my splitting head for a while.

All of my memories shortly after I arrived here were little more than half-truths or wishful thinking: my knowledge of bookbinding, my colleagues, the reason Marion left me, my daughter, msrip...

Was that my version of me as if I had never joined the Society of Thoth? Was that the function of the enemy's device, to erase or suppress all of my experiences concerning my membership? That seems, I don't know, frightfully specific. I mean, why destroy valuable information concerning your opposition?

Christ. I had to lie down for a few minutes. Head hurt so much, but it is a little better now.

The code word was at the bottom of the well, on the door to the museum: UTOPIANS. For that is what we are.

In any case, off to The World. I can not finish this trial fast enough. I want to go home.

Jan. 28th, 2005 12:52 pm Entry 106

I recall the day Robin posed for the statue, msrip. I remember scowling as the stonecrafter adjusted the single swath of silk that lie between my (twenty year-old) baby and the rest of God's Creation. I told her I was there purely for "moral support", but in truth I was deucedly uncomfortable with the idea of her posing nearly naked as The World. It had been her idea, though. Truly, what was a father to do. She was an adult as well as a productive member of her father's secret society.

I had forgotten, until today, just how much she had followed in my footsteps. And no wonder; I pressed her to excel from the moment she drew her first breath. Hell, I cut her bloody cord myself (which set the tone of my relationship with both females, in hindsight).

Now, there she is. Carved in unnatural detail from blushing stone, wrapped in a ribbon of rock barely preserving her modesty, she reaches out in evident joy to the universe around her. She stands weightlessly on one toe, as if the rapture of her awareness alone is canceling dim, dour gravity.

Standing impassively to her side is my doppelganger.

He watches as I write this; a twin, he is now identical in almost every way. A tic still rides one eye, perhaps, and I notice his breath is clear in the cold, thin atmosphere of Aerie, while clouds flow frigidly from my lungs. Otherwise, he possesses precisely the same build and composure as I. His muttering has ceased. He merely regards me dispassionately from thirty f

No, damn, twenty feet. He must have moved while I was writing. He is still silent as a ghost, but his gaze is intense, like a cat watching a spirit. He meets my glare firmly, neither judging nor offering the least amount of comfort.

The light is hurting my eyes. Wish I could write with them closed. My head hurts so badly it is as if my skull were cushioned in ground glass. If I keep it still the pain recedes to a stony ache, however, so my attention alternates like a rusty switch between the page and the damn corpse that has been haunting me ever since the Guard Post.

Now I can hear him, hear him move slowly toward me as the pain cuts a jigsaw into my retinas, I'm writing anything, furiously, listening to the blasted creature get closer and closer and closer.

God damn it he is right there, right there in front of me I can see his feet, his tattered shoes almost toe to toe. I can't stand to move my head but I can feel his breath on my hair. hes wearing away at something in my head, cracking it, no I won't, cracking it, eggshell thin, break tou all right I remember I can remember stop it I remember I cant I know I know IKNOWIKNOWIKN

Jan. 29th, 2005 09:16 am Entry 107

If you are a friend and you have read this far, it is possible you can forgive me. I may want to go home, now, or maybe I finally finished what I had set out to do all those months ago. In either case, please try to locate me, even if it is merely for revenge, or to bury the body. I imagine I could use the company.

I write these few remaining pages sitting in an overgrown garden, next to a quaint, cozy little white house. Scattered about me like an audience of old gnomes are orange pumpkins in varying states of decay.

Full circle.

Yesterday, standing over my doppelganger as it writhed in pain, I bent down and picked up this journal from where he had dropped it. My breath began to steam in the frigid air as his became invisible. Gradually, the rest of him followed, fading unevenly until only the eyes remained, twitching. Then those, too, disappeared as the delusion they were.

It has all come back to me, of course. It had been trying to since early on... since before I first dreamt of my double. I can see that, now.

I had blamed myself for the death of my daughter, msrip. She had not died in some random home invasion, as I had previously written, but had run to my residence in desperate escape from my enemies. Had I been home, she would still be breathing, but I was not and she had been cornered and killed.

I remember, now, my murderous rage at my enemies—a faction in a secret war that hid from the eyes of an ignorant, mundane world. I recall my anger turning to grief... turning into a heartsick impotence... becoming a disgust over the path down which I had forced my dear daughter... dissolving my soul until I could no longer bear to look at myself in a mirror.

I existed for a few years in that manner: empty, gutted, revisiting each "what if" that by then had planted deep taproots into my troubled mind. The power I had studied decades for, the mystical abilities that had set me and my brethren far apart from the common crowd, those magics faded as I withdrew into myself, quashing the arrogant sorcerer within until he could but gnash his teeth deep within my hollow heart.

With him out of the way, I could take the final step.

I left an anonymous tip for Our Opposition to find suggesting a major enemy agent was ready to call it quits and defect. I knew such a juicy plum would be irresistible, so I figured I had a mere hour before the knock on the door, the suspicious questions, the brutal abduction. I had no intention of letting them take me, of course; as I no longer had the courage to destroy myself, I figured I would go out in a blaze of miserable glory and let Them do the job for me. Suicide by cop, glorified.

Disaster struck. As I sat in a darkened, innominate apartment, footsteps signaled the arrival of strangers far sooner than I had anticipated. Had I underestimated the enemy? Were they more efficient, or bolder, than I had given credit? No. Instead, three of my friends, my compatriots-in-conspiracy, had learned of the "anonymous tip" and had sought to warn me of the impending attack.

Beside myself, I wasted valuable minutes insisting on my safety. I did my level best to convince my rescuers first that I was in no trouble, then that no such transparent tip would fool the opposition, and at last that I was up to whatever enemy action could deliver.

Ah, but my friends were no fools. They knew I was in overwhelming danger and that I had been suffering badly from Robin's death, msrip, and was not perhaps up to fending off a concentrated assault. Maybe... just maybe, they suspected more than that but, if so, they hid it well.

My world had fallen into deeper nightmare, my plan into ruin. Mad with guilt, I abruptly changed tactics and hustled my ignorant saviors down the stairs and toward my car. Erica, one of the three, went to retrieve a knapsack from her own car while I impatiently started the engine of mine. When she returned, her face had gone pale.

"I can't be certain, but I think they saw me."

Her voice had been thickened with fear. I barely waited until she was inside before I gunned the car wildly out of the parking lot and deep into traffic. When I had asked what could have been so important that she had risked being spotted, she revealed her possession of the Ivory Deck.

Her confession had startled me. The Ivory Deck was a major artifact of our organization. She had jeopardized her standing within the Society by merely removing it from its sanctum. She had taken it knowing how much danger I was in, but none of us dared use it unless in dire trouble indeed. As an escape, it was to be a last resort.

How funny it came to be exactly that.

I imagine you can piece together the rest, but let me spell something out to whomever is reading this: the "cop" of my dream, of my abused mind—that agent had neither intention nor ability to alter my memories so profoundly. All he had done was attempt to capture a highly-placed, exceedingly dangerous (as far as anyone knew) officer of the enemy. When said enemy, me, raised an unknown, possibly powerful artifact in a threatening manner, the ersatz policeman carried out his alternate orders.

He shot me between the eyes with his ordinary, perfectly deadly pistol. Or tried to; the Deck had been in the way.

I can only imagine the Ivory Deck had been shattered in the process. When my full memory returned yesterday, included in the flood of shameful information was the knowledge that there IS no "magic password" to leave here, this dimensional construction. When properly working, the Ivory Deck remains with the invoker. The fact that it had not this time meant that it must have been destroyed just as I had activated it. Intending to take everyone with me, I had succeeded only in transporting myself—and violently at that.

The botched translation into this mystical environment had fragmented my already injured mind. I figure my traumatized personality took that grand opportunity to save its own life by erasing everything that made it want to die.

This entire time I had been fighting against myself. I had been struggling so desperately, so valiantly all this while to regain an identity intent on committing suicide.

It is something I still need to decide upon, I suppose. Until such time as I make that choice, however, I shall explore these amazing realms in which I find myself so... perfectly entrapped.

Find me if you can.